12/6   FAN

love your
library

Buckinghamshire Libraries

Search, renew or reserve online 24/7
www.buckscc.gov.uk/libraries

24 hour renewal line
0303 123 0035

Enquiries
0845 230 3232

D1514156

15 252 370 4

Also by John Birmingham

Axis of Time
Weapons of Choice
Designated Targets
Final Impact

The Disappearance
Without Warning
After America
Angels of Vengeance

Stalin's Hammer: Rome

John Birmingham

momentum

First published by Momentum in 2012
Pan Macmillan Australia Pty Ltd
1 Market Street, Sydney 2000

A CIP record for this book is available at the National Library of
Australia

Stalin's Hammer: Rome

EPUB format: 9781743340769
Mobi format: 9781743340783
Print on Demand format: 9781743341391

Cover design by XOU Creative
Edited by Jon Gibbs
Proofread by Glenda Downing
Map by Laurie Whiddon

Macmillan Digital Australia: www.macmillandigital.com.au

To report a typographical error, please email
errors@momentumbooks.com.au

Visit www.momentumbooks.com.au to read more about all our books
and to buy books online. You will also find features, author interviews
and news of any author events.

Prologue

Joseph Stalin knew he was being watched. He closed his eyes and adjusted the soft, red blanket that covered his legs, like a child hiding under his bed covers, thinking that if he could not see the monster, the monster could not see him. The sun was warm on his face, and bright, through his paper-thin eyelids. Sitting there in his wheelchair, his face turned up, eyes closed, it was possible to imagine the whole world was a pink, warm womb.

He let his chin slowly fall to his chest before opening his eyes and turning his glare on Beria. "We are delayed, Lavrenty Pavlovich. To what end?"

Stalin patted his pockets, looking for his old pipe, forgetting that he had not smoked in years. The doctors had said it would kill him. Frustrated at the delay, frustrated at the doctors, angry that he could not enjoy a simple pipe, his scowl grew darker. Once upon a time the hardest men in Russia had quailed at the sight of him playing with that pipe. To turn it this way and that, to stroke the bowl with his thumb while never moving to pack even one shred of tobacco in there – that was enough to signal his displeasure. Enough to make strong men quiver with fear. Now when he patted his pockets, he just looked like an old cripple, forgetful and failing.

Still, what little colour Beria had in his face leached away at the thunderous look on Stalin's. That was something.

"No delay. There is no delay, comrade. Everything is running to schedule."

The chief of the Functional Projects Bureau stammered over his last words and nervously checked the iPad he carried. A rare and valuable working model, an Apple original, one of the last before the 'flex' models debuted, and salvaged from the emergence of the British stealth destroyer way back in 1942, it was still sleeker and more powerful than anything Functional Projects had managed to produce. Then again, it was also vastly more elegant and powerful than any of the cheaper Samsung or Google flexipads they had also salvaged.

Stalin waved him off with a backhanded gesture. "Gah. Enough excuses, Lavrenty Pavlovich. Begin the demonstration. I have many days of travel to return to Moscow. Push your buttons. Bring down the sky. Be done with it."

"The satellite is almost in position now," Beria assured him. "We must retire inside."

His bodyguard leaned forward. "Vozhd?" he asked, seeking permission to move him.

"Yes, yes," said Stalin, who did not really want to give up his place in the sun. The winters grew longer as he grew older. He was certain of it. He enjoyed the mild spring weather, but soon enough, too soon, the leaves on the small stand of trees outside his apartment back in the Kremlin would turn red again, then gold, then brown as winter stalked back into the land. What did those books say? The ones his daughter loved, from the broken future. Winter was coming? His last perhaps. He adjusted the blanket again – an old habit, it had not moved – and tried to not let his disappointment show as his guard wheeled him off the terrace out of the sun and back inside the bunker.

He felt the chill as soon as they passed into the shadows of the deep concrete passageway. Solid iron blast doors rumbled behind him as the small party of high officials, bureaucrats and technicians filed in, trudging in procession to the bunker from which they would monitor the test. Moisture leaked from the thick concrete walls, giving Stalin pause to worry about his arthritis. He regretted having insisted on traveling all the way out here to witness the test firing for himself. Then he smiled. Beria undoubtedly regretted it more, and that was cause for some mild amusement. Stalin knew his deputy premier would be fretting now, squirming inside like a greasy little weasel, anxious that nothing should go wrong.

The tension in the control room was tangible. He could feel it on his skin, taste it even at the back of his mouth. It was a familiar taste, of a fine vintage. He had been supping on men's fear for so long now he believed he could take some nourishment from it. The scientists and military officers – no, they were NKVD Spetsnaz; Beria's thralls, not Red Army, he reminded himself – all did their best to avoid catching his gaze. Beria scuttled about, snapping and hissing at the technical staff, his spidery white fingers stabbing so hard at the screen of the iPad that Stalin thought he might punch it to the floor. That would be amusing.

His bodyguard – it was Yagi today – wheeled him past banks of computer terminals, monitoring screens, and control boards dense with flashing lights and illuminated buttons. The supreme leader of the Soviet Union understood none of it. The technology was all plundered from the far and impossible future, the world that could not be.

He would never see that particular future. He knew that, of course. Accepted it. Life ebbed away from him now – in spite of all the new "miracle" medical treatments and organ therapies, life itself retreated from Joseph Stalin on a quickening tide of years and minutes. But nobody else would see the future from whence Kolhammer and his international fleet had Emerged either, because *he* would not let it come to pass. *He* would not let it be, this false future where Putinist thugs and bandits ruled the Rodina, where the revolution was mocked and mourned. And dead.

It would not be.

At a word from him, as long as Beria had done his job, the sky would fall in on the world outside this bunker, and the real future would draw that much closer. Yagi brought him to a stop a few feet from the viewing port created especially for him. The armored glass was 7 inches thick, they had told him, and the reinforced concrete wall of the bunker at least 3 feet deep. Peering through this personal viewport was a little like looking down a short tunnel. The glass distorted the view somewhat, and gave it a dark green tinge. Steel shutters stood ready to slam down if needed, but he could not see them. Nobody could. Only a wheelchair-bound Stalin and one of the technicians, who was a dwarf, were of a height to have an unimpeded view through the port. Everybody else had to make do with the viewing screens. There were dozens of them about, but the two largest ones hung from the wall directly in front of him, above the viewing slit.

The room was chilly, because of all the infernal computers, which always seemed to be in danger of overheating. The cold, stale, recycled air irritated his eyes and seeped into his bones, but it awoke his senses, and he did want to see this. It was why he had traveled so far east, beyond the natural barrier of the mountains.

Involuntarily he glanced upwards, imagining American satellites prowling overhead, peering down on him. But there was only the low ceiling of un-rendered cement. And above that – tons of rock.

"You are sure Kolhammer is not watching this on some television in the White House?" he growled at Beria. "They are always watching us."

Startled out of some reverie, the NKVD boss jumped a little, and even squeaked. He was more nervous than usual. "We have done our best, our utmost, to draw their attention away from the proving grounds," he said, stammering as before. "Ten Red Army divisions and fraternal bloc forces are exercising as close to the Oder as we dare. There have been incidents. I made sure of that personally. What satellite cover they do not have watching us there will be trained on Admiral Koniev's newly unmasked fleet base. Our strategic forces are ready to test fire a fusion warhead to mask the geologic signal. This is all settled, Vozhd. By your very self."

Stalin waved him away again, a stock gesture when dealing with Beria. He knew everything the man had just said, but he wanted him to repeat it. If Beria's plan to mask the Hammer Fall test failed, Comrade Beria would pay the price. Not Stalin.

Klaxons and sirens began to sound all around them, and somewhere in the distance he heard the deep, bass rumble of more blast doors sliding into place. The countdown clock between the two large viewing screens clicked over to ten minutes.

In spite of his weariness and his age – he should have been dead two years now – in spite of all that he had done and seen, Joseph Stalin could not help but feel a flicker of excitement in his chest. Well, hopefully it was just excitement … After his last heart attack, the doctors had told him (or rather suggested, very mildly) that he might need to think about cutting back to one serving each day of his favorite lamb stew. He wiggled his fingers now, marveling at how old his hands looked, how skeletal and heavily veined.

1953, he thought.

These hands through which his blood still flowed, with which he could still touch the world, they should have clawed at the last moments of life in 1953. On March 5 – as a massive stroke shredded his brain and twisted his body into a crippled, piss-stained mess.

He smiled at the thought. He was still here. For now. Inside, he still felt like a twenty-year-old revolutionary, but his body was failing him. Even with his blood washed clean by a fresh, transplanted liver, even with improbably tiny machines regulating his heartbeat and sweeping toxins from his body, it was failing him. He should have been used to it, he supposed. So many had failed him over the decades. Their bodies, at least, he could pile up like cordwood. His own, he was stuck with, mostly, despite the efforts of his transplant surgeons and pharmacists.

The Vozhd had simply given too much to the struggle over the years. That was why he was so excited and intrigued by the possibilities of today's test. Since the reactionary Kolhammer forces had Emerged from the Gordian knot of history at the Battle of Midway, Joseph Stalin had lived every day with the knowledge that he had limited time to set history right, to secure the revolution, and his place in it.

Emerged from history, and destroyed it, he thought. Destroyed the settled history of the twentieth century, and the twenty-first century after that. It was still a wonder to him how nobody in the West could see the obvious truth of it. How the very impossibility of Admiral Kolhammer's arrival from the year 2021 through this 'wormhole' spoke to the impossibility of the future from which he had come.

He grunted in frustration, setting off a momentary panic amongst his hangers-on, but he ignored them.

The forces of history operate like a machine, he thought, as technicians and dogsbodies fussed about him. History: driving human progress from barbarity to civilization, from the feudal to the capitalist, and then inevitably on to the final socialist stages. A history in which the USSR fell was simply not possible. Reality was not engineered in such a fashion. Thus history had righted itself with the destructive miracle of the Emergence.

Or rather, it had started to right itself. The revolutionary work of men was in the hands of men, of course. Stalin hoped that today they would come one crucial step closer to completing that work.

"Two minutes, Vozhd," said Beria, surprising him.

Where had the time gone? Stalin shook his head, disgusted. He had been daydreaming again. He leaned forward to peer out through the armored glass. A nameless valley fell away from them hundreds of feet below, disappearing into the haze. Ten miles away, hundreds of obsolete tanks and trucks, many of them salvaged from the battlefields of the Great Patriotic War, waited on the valley floor. He was aware of increased tension behind him as the technicians hurried through their last-minute procedures. Literally – the last-minute procedures. The countdown clock had reached sixty seconds. Beria really had nothing to do, setting himself to annoy everyone with his pestering and interference as he did it.

"Leave them alone, Lavrenty Pavlovich!" Stalin ordered. "Let them do their duty."

Chastened, the chief engineer – *Pah, that was a laugh!* – of the Functional Projects Bureau quit bustling around and hovering at the shoulders of his senior men. He opened and closed the cover of his flexipad a number of times, before setting it down on a steel workbench and shuffling over to stand beside Stalin.

"There is nothing left to do but wait," he said.

"Then we shall wait," replied the Vozhd.

The final countdown was strangely disappointing. A disembodied voice on the public address system took them through the last few seconds: "*Three ... two ... one ... launch ...*" But of course there were no rockets to roar or shake the earth beneath their feet.

"How long?" asked Stalin.

Beria seemed unnaturally pleased to have a question he could answer promptly. "Less than two minutes," he said with confidence. "These are the small, tactical rods we are testing today. They will launch from low orbit and accelerate to 9000 meters per second."

Stalin scowled at him, stealing some of that confidence away. "And we are safe here in this bunker?"

"Oh yes," said Beria, with apparent relief. "We would not dare test the largest of the rods like this. They are designed to reduce mountains, such as this, to smoking craters."

"Like Tunguska?"

Beria hesitated, as though it were a trick question. Which in a way it was. The scientists and engineers – real scientists and real engineers, unlike Beria – had briefed him well at the start of this project. They had to. It was a massive investment of the state's resources, and one that drew money and men away from one of Stalin's pet projects: the electronic storage of human memory and consciousness. His gaze faltered for a moment, slipping away from Beria to stare at the back of his old, liver-spotted hands again.

"Vozhd?"

"Pah! Do not bother," Stalin told him, worried that his mind had wandered again. "I know about Tunguska. I know how it was different. The rock from space – a giant snowball, they told me – it exploded in the air. These rods will not."

"No," said Beria. "Look ..." He bent his knees and leaned forward, pointing toward the viewing aperture, even though the giant screens hanging above it afforded a grand, God-like view of the entire valley.

The dictator peered out through the armored-glass slit but found himself watching the screens too. They had split into windows to display the video feeds from a dozen cameras scattered up and down the valley. None of the hundreds of tanks, trucks and APCs out there were moving; they sat warmed by the afternoon sun. Stalin opened his mouth to say something when he thought he spotted a flight of birds sweeping across the scene, but before he could form the words, bright white streaks of light speared down from the sky. He saw the flash of impact through the glass just a moment before the very planet heaved and rumbled in shock. His mouth dropped open in surprise as the roaring noise of impact and detonation reached deep inside the bunker.

There was little and less to see on the screens, which didn't so much blank out as "white out". He squinted involuntarily before turning his attention back to the viewing port. Beria too had bent over again to look through it, as other men and women, some in uniform and some in coveralls and lab coats, did the same. A few flinched away, as an enormous fireball raced up the valley toward them. Stalin thought he could make out the pressure wave that preceded it, flattening the sea of grass and a few small saplings that stood between the foot of the mountain bunker and the point of impact.

Then heavy steel shutters slammed down, blocking off even that view. A few people jumped. But not the supreme leader of the Soviet people. He closed his eyes and imagined the sun, warm on his face, and bright even through his eyelids.

01

May 6, 1955: South Rome (Allied sector)

"Your Highness," said the actor, as he performed a short bow. "It is an honor."

Harry was surprised by how much richer Sir Alec Guinness's voice was in person, how much power and subtlety had been pressed out of it by the primitive recording technologies of the mid twentieth century. At least, the first time around. The invited guests and attendant media for the movie premiere were packed tightly into the art deco foyer of the Cinema Barberini, and the crowded space roared with many hundreds of voices – especially Italian voices, which tended toward amplified stridency at the quietest of times anyway. Even so, Harry had no trouble making out the actor's words. Unlike him, Harry was forced to use his parade-ground holler to cut through the cacophony.

"Sir Alec," he boomed, "the honor is all mine. Love your work."

Guinness smiled and shook Harry's proffered hand. Both men had strong, calloused grips, but neither felt the need for anything as gauche as a bone-crushing competition. In Harry's experience of 1950s society, that made for a pleasant change.

"I'm never quite sure how to take it when people say something like that these days," said the recently knighted actor. "Would it be presumptuous of me to ask whether you refer to my old work or my new?"

Harry almost blundered into a Star Wars fan-boy moment, but Guinness was famously touchy on the subject of his uptime portrayal of Obi-Wan. *Better to stick with the classics*, Harry thought, as a waiter bearing a tray of champagne, wine and spirits somehow managed to slip through the crush around them. Hundreds of guests, all in formal wear, most of them smoking and all of them drinking, pressed in from all sides.

"Well, my grandmother was always a big fan of your George Smiley," he said, almost shouting above the din. "But I'd say that your Prince Harry puts them all in the shade."

It was a lie, of course, but one that brought forth a spirited laugh from Sir Alec.

"Well, my Prince Harry is not a patch on yours," replied Guinness. "But it was a jolly romp of a film to make after that disastrous bloody *Hamlet* at the New Theatre. How I managed to fall into that trap for a second time I will never know."

Resplendent in regimental formal wear, Harry felt hot under the bright lights, and sweat trickled down the small of his back. He threw down most of his drink – a soda water tricked up to look like a gin and tonic – in a couple of urgent gulps. Long before he had arrived in June 1942, he had learned to be careful about drinking alcohol in public; although he had also learned that people and, more importantly the press, seemed to care much less about such things here than they had back up whence he had come.

"I imagine you thought forewarned was forearmed," he said after finishing his sparkling water. "You wouldn't be alone in making that mistake."

"Touché, Your Highness."

Harry had some trouble reconciling the fit, young actor standing in front of him with the old, limping man he recalled from the first of the Star Wars films. But he had no trouble imagining how Sir Alec Guinness had found himself caught up in a disastrous theatrical misadventure, even though he had been warned off by his own future history, delivered by Harry and 10,000 other uptimers from 2021. Sometimes being told of the mistakes you were about to make was less of a warning and more of a provocation – as the Nazis had found out.

On the other hand, thought Harry, catching sight of Sophia Loren gossiping with Errol Flynn on the other side of the room, there were plenty who had managed to avoid their fates. Or at least their fates as Harry knew of them. Flynn over there, for instance, had already undergone the surgery that would save him from a heart attack a couple of years from now. He looked dangerously healthy, having given up the booze and smokes as well. And a couple of months of SAS-style fitness training to play opposite Guinness in *Capture von Braun!* hadn't hurt either. Harry liked Flynn, but he had to wonder why the film's producers had chosen the Australian to play Captain Marcel Ronsard of the Free French 1st Army.

Well, actually he didn't have to wonder about that at all. This was Hollywood, after all, or Britain's version of it. So the raid on the German rocket facility at Donzenac in France, a mission nearly eight months in the planning and execution, was compressed into just over an hour and a half on screen, with an Australian playing the token French officer, and Mademoiselle Anjela Claudel of the Bureau des Opérations Aériennes portrayed by the Italian actress Sophia Loren. At least Flynn's mustache looked French, he supposed.

A bell began to ring: time for the audience to move into the theater and take their seats. Immediately the background buzz and rumble of conversation seemed to get louder. Harry noted the sudden flare of dozens of cigarette lighters firing up as their owners rushed to hammer in one last coffin nail.

"Are you going in?" he asked, as Sir Alec looked around for a waiter to unburden him of the drink he had hardly touched.

"Oh, yes. I'm sure if you could fight your way into a secret Nazi rocket base to blow up their whizz-bangs and kidnap their boffins, I can at least sit through the whole lark in the comfort of the Barberini. Besides, I haven't actually seen the finished version yet."

"Allow me," said Harry, taking Guinness's unwanted drink from him and palming it off on a waitress passing behind the actor. "I'm one up on you in that case. We had a sneak preview at the palace last week. Nana loved it. Thought it was very exciting. Although, I notice they didn't have Ms. Loren slitting anyone's throat for making a nuisance of themselves. Not in this version, anyway."

For just a moment, it looked as though a shadow passed across Sir Alec's face. He looked Harry in the eye as he spoke. "People who have not played at war, sir, have no idea what an ugly, wretched game it is. I wonder sometimes whether we let them down by not telling them truthfully."

"But war's a game," said Harry, "which, were their subjects wiser, Kings would not play at." The smile did not reach his eyes.

"Cowper, I believe."

"Could be," admitted Harry, "but I read it in Freddy Forsyth."

"And you, Your Highness, not tempted by a second viewing?" Guinness asked with a slightly mischievous grin.

"Duty calls," Harry replied. "Well – a very early supper first, then duty."

The bell rang again and the jostling crush of the crowd became a slow-moving tide, flowing toward the doors of the theater. As the invitees, in their black-tie outfits and heavy-looking cocktail dresses, gradually shuffled past the two men, the large press contingent, those without their own invitations at any rate, were left behind. Harry nodded at a small clutch of women. Resplendent in formal wear, they were engrossed in their devices, running jeweled fingers across glass screens. One of the women shook her device and thumped it against her thigh before returning to the inviting, exclusive glow of a white screen. The networks were good in Rome, a function of the heavy Allied military and administrative presence, but they were still unreliable to anyone who remembered the future.

Harry felt his own iPhone Ultima, a civilian model he'd shepherded carefully through the years, vibrate in his breast pocket. One of the women looked up, her face impassive while her eyes revealed what was waiting on the phone.

"I have a date," he said, conspiratorially leaning in toward Guinness. "A rather impatient one, I am afraid."

"I see. In my day, a mere glance was sufficient," teased Sir Alec, having heard the buzz of Harry's phone. "Well, as critical and defining a cultural moment as is the premiere of *Capture von Braun!*, I do recognize that there are more important things in the world. You must be about your business, Your Highness. If I might be so bold, however," he added, "which one is she?"

Harry couldn't help but smile. "The tall, dark-haired woman, the American in the white dress."

"Miss ... I'm sorry *Ms.* Duffy," said the actor, correcting himself. "I thought as much. I had observed her watching you these last few minutes."

The crowd had thinned out to the point where the two men were able to speak in a more normal, conversational tone. Harry was impressed, if a little horrified, at the thick fog of cigarette smoke that remained in their wake. Sir Alec must've been possessed of especially sharp vision to pick out Julia Duffy through the crowd and the smokescreen.

"Do you know her?"

"Not personally," replied Guinness, "but she did interview me a few weeks ago in connection with the film. She struck me as one of the more intelligent and perceptive reporters it's ever been my displeasure to talk to." He smiled as he said it.

"Tough interview, eh?"

"Indeed. She was very well informed about the failure of my theater venture, and not at all reluctant to keep asking me the most discomfiting questions about it."

The bell began to ring again, a little more urgently, summoning the final stragglers. Harry watched a couple of publicists consulting their handhelds. Contemporary models. One pressed a clunky flip phone to his head with a numbered knob clearly visible on its backside, while the other consulted something like a cross between an original Star Trek clipboard and a first gen Palm Pilot. The gadgets looked huge and cumbersome, but for anyone without privileged access to genuine uptime tech, they were cutting edge; like the first-gen digital watch Star Trek guy consulted impatiently as the two made their way over to wrangle Sir Alec away.

"Sorry about that," said Harry with bluff good humor as he patted Guinness on the shoulder. "In my experience, when dealing with Julia it's best to just lie back and think of England."

Sir Alec snorted just as the first of the publicists arrived, a short, rotund man with heavily oiled hair, wringing his hands nervously.

"Your Highness, Sir Alec ..."

"If you could just spare us a moment," said the actor, politely enough, but with enough steel in his voice that Harry could easily imagine him commanding a small boat running weapons to partisans in the Balkans during the war.

The publicist coughed and nodded, and backed away. "Of course, of course ..."

Harry's breast buzzed again. He resisted the urge to grope for his phone.

"I would not want you to think me uncharitable about your lady friend," continued Sir Alec. "She really was very good at her job. Unfortunately, that made for a rather uncomfortable time for me. But, of course, I brought that on myself. Lessons of history, and everything. And I will say, of all the interviews I sat through to publicize this film, hers was the only one that didn't bring up that bloody *Star Wars* movie. Please do pass on my regards."

His breast poket buzzed a third time. Harry bowed his head briefly. "I will. And for what it's worth, I really did enjoy this movie. We all did."

"Very kind of you to say so," said Guinness. "But now I can see from the panic sweat soaking the armpits of my press relations professional over there that I must away. Enjoy your date, and please, my compliments to Ms. Duffy."

"Of course."

They shook hands again and parted as Sir Alec was ushered away, not toward the theater but into the clutches of yet more journalists for another round of interviews.

Harry stifled a sigh as he spotted his own personal protection detail – two special constables from Scotland Yard dressed in dark double-breasted suits, both of them wearing homburgs. At least they would keep a discreet distance this evening, but Harry could not help feeling slightly put out. He was much more able to take care of himself than these two. For that matter, Julia Duffy was probably a more daunting prospect to any would-be attacker than the plain-clothes bobbies.

She had his attention now, smiling at last and waving as she said goodbye to her colleagues. They were very obviously reporters as well. They carried notebooks and large satchels slung over their shoulders, from which one of the women took out a small cardboard camera to snap Harry's photo as he approached. Julia backhanded the woman in the solar plexus, playfully, but firmly enough to drive a small '*oof*' from her, after which the little cardboard camera disappeared.

Julia, he noted, was not carrying a satchel full of disposable Kodaks. She was packing a 21C digital shooter. Her old Canon Eos, he was certain. Nearly a quarter of a century old, and still one of the most advanced pieces of optic technology marooned here in the 1950s. A lot of people would think it foolish, a woman hauling around such a valuable piece of kit. Especially in a city like Rome, where the Allied sector still swarmed with displaced people ten years after the end of the war. Harry knew better, however. His on-and-off girlfriend was an embed, with nearly as much combat experience as him. A common street thief who tried knocking her down for the camera was more likely to leave the encounter with a couple of bullets in his face or a knife buried deep in his neck.

"Hey," she called out. "You done schmoozing with all your fancy actor friends? Got time for a drink with a working girl?"

Julia's companions fell silent as he drew near. Harry revised his previous opinion about them: they probably weren't uptimers. Too young, for a start. They were dressed in the lighter, more casual fashion of the next century, and styled their hair and makeup to imitate Julia's own; but they did not have her hard, angular body shape. Even in her forties, her figure remained gym-ripped and almost masculine compared to the soft, doughy shapes of women from this era. Her musculature was well defined and very apparent

19

when she moved. Theirs was not. Their cheeks retained the fleshy curves of cherubs. Diet and brutal exercise had stripped most of the body fat from Duffy, and it showed in her high cheekbones and in the slightly hollow panes of her face. The temps' aping of her uptime style did not extend to Paleo diets, MMA workouts and high-intensity interval training. When they spoke, to say hello, they did so with American accents and he was finally able to place them.

California. The Zone.

02

May 6, 1955: North Rome (Soviet sector)

Twelve hours earlier

The church, a humble box of gray brick and slate and narrow, unglazed windows, sat on the point of a sharp turn in a nest of backstreets and alleyways a few blocks north of the Vatican. Ivanov peered through one of the slits, scanning the cobblestone passage outside their hiding place in the weak, gray light of morning. Overnight a sewer had backed up nearby and flooded the alley with a shallow stream of excrement. Unpleasant, but useful. It meant that foot traffic, already light in this part of the Soviet sector, was unlikely to build up as the Romans took to the streets.

It meant the chances of the mission playing out in his favor were just that little bit better.

Today that mission was a man called Valentin Sobeskaia. A Russian businessman, and a *boyar* of the Party, free to travel to Rome for the GATT talks. And not just to the Soviet-controlled quadrant either; Sobeskaia was trusted enough to be able to cross over to Free Rome, the Allied sector. Free to cross over, but not free to move around without an escort or constraints. In "free", South Rome, the NKVD would guard and watch him, holding him as closely as a newborn. Ironically, it was safer and much easier for Ivanov to contact him here, through his mistress, Anya, in the open-air prison of the city's Communist-controlled north.

The special forces veteran scanned the streets outside again. Nothing moved.

Normal life, such as it was, was possible just a few short streets away, on the other side of the Roman Wall. Here in the Soviet-controlled sector, however, there were no privately owned *trattoria* or *ristorante*, no crowded bars hot and bright with life and celebration. There were "people's canteens", where you might get a drink if your tastes ran to toe-curling Bulgarian wine and thin, oily Moskovskaya vodka, but they were poorly patronized by the Romans. Only the lowest, most despised cadre of Party members were to be found there. Even the poorly paid junior officers of the occupying Red Army divisions avoided the canteens, preferring to eat and drink in their barracks. It was safer that way. A man was less likely to get a shiv in the neck or turn up floating down the Tiber with his belly sliced open and his innards trailing behind him.

"Five minutes," Franco warned him.

Ivanov granted him a curt, "Thank you." Franco Furedi, a trigger man from a minor but rising family of La Cosa Nostra, had guided him into the Soviet sector and hopefully would guide him out again. The common courtesy of a thank-you here and there was not simply good manners but good policy, in Ivanov's experience. Especially with the mafia. They took the proprieties seriously.

He scoped out what little he could see of their target building, about 100 yards away, before pulling back from the window. It was dark enough inside the church that he fitted his night-vision goggles before stepping away from the window. The Trident Optics 4G headset was nowhere near as advanced as the satellite-linked combat goggles he'd worn back up in the twenty-first, but these were as good as accelerated 1950s technology got – and that was pretty fucking good, he had to admit. They were the most advanced piece of equipment he carried under the Wall in a small canvas satchel. Unfortunately, he had no live comms link or electronic overwatch on this mission. He would have to make do with his own eyes and ears. And with Franco, of course. His ally of convenience.

With the Trident's low light amplification mode powered up, the simple, unadorned interior of the little church emerged in lime-green luminescence around him. The Communists had boarded up the building years ago, as they had with so many in their sector of Rome. Not every church had been shut down, of course. Soviet dominion was ten years young in this part of the city and throughout the north of Italy. The ailing Stalin had not yet consolidated his rule to the point where he could glibly sweep aside 2000 years of culture and history, no matter how much his natural inclination would have been to do just that. And so for now, many churches remained open, but they tended to be the larger cathedrals, where the congregation could be observed en masse, and where the officiating clergy needed the approval of the Communist regime to practice. Attendance at these state-approved places of worship had been falling away for years. Exactly as planned, Ivanov noted. Most people, he knew, worshiped privately in their homes, tended to by priests who worked secretly, without state sanction, risking their freedom and occasionally their lives to do so.

Franco's brother, Marius, was one such man. His SIS file was surprisingly thick for a humble Catholic priest, although Ivanov was frustrated and impressed in equal measure to find there were few photographs of the man, and what images the secret service did have were at least fifteen years old. Father Marius was a holy spirit indeed. (British intelligence, unlike their cousins across the pond, still kept most of their records on paper. They said it was to avoid the sort of breaches that had become commonplace uptime, but everyone in the business knew they simply did not have the budget that the Office of Strategic Services enjoyed for information technology.) Ivanov was familiar with the British and American files on the Furedi brothers, and the networks for which the two men toiled. The Trimbole family in Franco's case; the Vatican's ad hoc security apparatus for his brother.

Presumably there was another file, at least on Marius, held somewhere within the local directorate of the NKVD. It was he who had provided the location of this abandoned and shuttered holy place that could be accessed via a buried part of the old city, a pitch-black warren of subterranean passages, catacombs, aqueducts and even intact but entombed buildings from the late Roman Republican era, about 200 years before the birth of Jesus Christ. A small world lost to time during one of the periodic eruptions of civil conflict that wracked the city and the Empire at that point.

All this Ivanov had second-hand from his guide. They never met with Franco's brother, who was away somewhere else in the north, on "the pontiff's business". The former Spetsnaz officer had no doubt that whatever the holier Furedi sibling was up to, it was almost certainly as dangerous as their mission this evening.

The other, less spiritually inclined Furedi had already fitted his own NVGs and was playing with the setting, switching between LLAMP mode and infrared.

"Low light is best," Ivanov said quietly, "especially when we get down below street level. Less drain on the battery, too."

"*Sì*, okay," Furedi answered.

Ivanov appreciated the man's ability to take an order, or at least a suggestion. He had known many soldiers to bristle when he pointed out the obvious to them. But the mafia man was in his mid to late forties and seemed content to take as much instruction from Ivanov as he could get. It was not surprising. The Russian's equipment was high spec and valuable. Furedi would not be allowed to keep the goggles once the mission was over – assuming they survived. But Ivanov knew from his long experience of working with insurgents that giving them access to this kind of equipment simply brought forward the day when they would acquire it for themselves. On that day, a man like Franco Furedi, a man with operational experience of its use, would find himself much valued by his overlords.

"It is time," said the Italian. A few quiet strides took him over to the window where Ivanov had stood vigil. After a final check of the street outside, he returned, collected the small backpack on the stone floor between them and led the way into the vestry.

Where the main body of the church had been empty but clean, if very dusty, the small room to the left of the altar space where the priests had once pre-pared for mass was strewn with rubble. Even using the goggles, picking a path through the shattered flag-stones and granite was hazardous. You couldn't trust your depth perception; it would always be just a notch off.

Both men carefully climbed over the debris to the far corner, to a small hole in the floor, just wide enough for Ivanov to squeeze through. Franco went down first. He was thin and agile enough to lower himself through the opening and drop into the dark-ness wearing his little backpack. They already knew that Ivanov, about twice his size through the shoulders and chest, would have a tight squeeze. The Russian dropped his satchel down before carefully lowering himself after it. He had been much larger, years ago, back when he still lived in the gym, pump-ing iron by day and vodka by night. Years on the move had made him considerably leaner, yet he was still an impressive-sized man. That, he knew, would be a problem in the Roman underground.

He felt Franco's hands grip his boots and guide them to a piece of unbroken ground. Or rather, un-broken roofline. An hour before, they had come up into the vestry by climbing onto the roof of an ancient temple, on top of which this church had been built, perhaps 1000 years ago. An archeologist could doubtless spend his entire career studying just this one small buried neighborhood, but for the special forces operator it was of interest primarily because of the hidden access it provided to their target.

Once he had regained his footing, Ivanov followed Franco across the temple of some long-dead god, or gods, crouching at one point to duck beneath the rough red bricks of the vaulted ceiling that had buried this part of the old city. A few feet ahead of him, Franco swung over a low line of carved stones with the assurance of a man who had done the same thing many times before.

A couple of cigarette butts, some discarded chocolate-bar wrappers and an empty fifth of Johnnie Walker, all scattered around the cold ashes of an old campfire in a small cleared area in front of the temple, spoke of previous visits. Ivanov wondered what business his mafia guide must have had with the Church that he should have been entrusted with such useful information.

There was virtually no ambient light down here, not even a few stray photons leaking down from the vestry.

"I am turning on my LEDs," he warned Franco.

"*Sì,*" Furedi replied.

The mafia soldier turned away from him, lest he be temporarily blinded. Ivanov thumbed the switch on his night-vision goggles, powering up a small cluster of light-emitting diodes. Instantly their surroundings sprang into bright relief. Ivanov squeezed his own eyes shut as the optical processors struggled for a second to adapt. After a moment, the gloomy subterranean scene was rendered in opalescent clarity.

The two men, dressed in the gray coveralls of municipal sanitation workers, stood in front of the collapsed remains of whatever building had once been a neighbor to the buried sepulcher beneath the old Roman Catholic church. The rubble provided a convenient series of stepping stones up to the roof. Ivanov's natural caution and years of experience demanded that he now survey the area for any change while they'd been topside. But the interred street remained as it had been from an hour earlier, as it had been for a millennium or more. Where once the citizens and slaves of Rome would have looked up into a hot blue Mediterranean sky, he now saw soil and roots and the scalloped brickwork of a vaulted ceiling that here and there gave way to flat slabs of granite and marble.

Franco's people had done some work toward clearing the street in front of the temple, of rock falls and shattered masonry, exposing the original paving stones in the process. But they had done so in order to provide themselves with a more convenient lay-up point, rather than out of any interest in ancient history. A few steps away, the cobblestones and pavers were lost again under centuries of soil build-up. It was one of the stranger places that Major Pavel Ivanov had been to; preserved well enough that were he given to flights of imagination, he could very easily have closed his eyes and filled this entombed district with hundreds of long-dead Romans, with priests and acolytes chanting in the temple, with snorting oxen dragging carts laden down with produce from surrounding farmlands as the Republican-era client mobs of the *optimates* and *populares* swarmed around them and legionaries stomped by, marching past in triumph – the only time soldiers were permitted in the city in full regalia.

Ivanov sometimes surprised himself, that he could remember so much from his academy days in a future lost to eternity. What were the Communists thinking – that they could just sweep away the crush of so much history and culture? Probably. Stalin had shown himself to be more than willing to eliminate whole peoples if they proved inconvenient. The Romans were not the Chechens or the Cossacks, however, and the spear point of six NATO divisions was poised just a few miles away in Frascati.

No, the great game would be played out here by different rules. There would be blood and terror, but it would be shed quietly in the shadows by men like him. Ten years worth of terror was painted onto the backs of his eyelids now. It made him warm, sick to his stomach, and a little dizzy.

"We go now," said Franco. "I lead."

"Of course," said Ivanov. Yes, this was his mission and ultimately he would make all the important decisions, but one of the first such decisions was to place his trust in this man who was, in the end, nothing more than the indentured assassin of a small, somewhat pathetic criminal oligarchy. A clan of thieves and killers that just happened to be the most important rival power to the Soviets and their local collaborators in this part of the eternal city.

Franco added the brightness of his own headset's LED cluster to Ivanov's, lighting up the bizarre surroundings as brilliantly as Piazza Navona on a festival night. The two men walked at a brisk pace through the empty, subterranean streetscape, slowing to climb and occasionally crawl over piles of rubble and earth that were otherwise impassable.

Ivanov was soon sweating with the exertion and found himself impressed again with Furedi's quiet, obdurate ability to press forward at a steady pace without complaint. He had put the man's age at just under fifty perhaps, although it was sometimes difficult with Italians because of the privations they had suffered through the war. Many of them, particularly in the larger cities, looked older and more worn out than would otherwise have been the case. Franco was gray-haired and hollow of cheek, with a mournful expression on his face most times. But he looked like a man whose hair had been silver from a young age and who had probably come into the world glaring at it with an evil eye. There was no questioning his fitness for this particular task, or his commitment. He had already put one body in the river while sneaking Ivanov into the Soviet sector. Furedi moved through the caverns and crawl-ways beneath Communist-controlled Rome with a surety and confidence that spoke of real familiarity.

"Down," he said, pointing at a drainage pipe that disappeared under the collapse of what looked to have been another ancient temple, this one considerably larger than the previous one.

The aperture was just big enough for Franco to be able to crouch deeply and shuffle into it without crawling. For Ivanov, the way through was not so easy, and he soon found himself on his hands and knees. He could hear water running in the distance and, after crawling for a few minutes, the dry dusty bricks beneath his hands grew moist and slimy. The stench of sewage was much stronger now.

The drainage pipe narrowed and soon Franco was also on his hands and knees, while Ivanov stretched out onto his stomach, inching forward slowly, pushing with his toes and elbows. The effluent on the crumbling brick walls of the old Roman drainage pipe was a blessing, reducing any friction he would have to fight against. He couldn't help but think of himself as a giant Russian turd being squeezed through the bowels of the city.

"Why you laugh? Is funny, this?" his guide asked as he pulled himself over the lip at the narrowest part of the pipe, eeling down into a much larger drain.

"Toilet humor," Ivanov deadpanned.

Franco nodded as if he understood exactly what the Russian meant. They pushed on for what felt like an eternity, the only communication between them an occasional grunt. Ivanov retreated from his immediate surrounds. He stopped thinking about how long it was taking them, how many hours they would have to crawl deeper and deeper under the old city. He especially did not dwell on the fact that he could not turn around, could not raise his head, could not really backtrack. He was like an animal in a burrow so deep and narrow that there was no choice but to push on, inching forward, hour after hour.

"We nearly here," Franco said at last, jutting his chin up at the curve of bricks above them as Ivanov prised himself out into the wider space with a great sense of relief.

A foul, contaminated stream of brown sludge ran a foot deep down the slight descent to the north-east. Huge black rats skittered and splashed away from them and the walls seethed with worms and cockroaches and all manner of unidentifiable insect life. Franco turned off the LED cluster on his goggles. The artificial illumination provided by Ivanov's headset was more than enough to light the way to their next objective, partly because a few shafts of weak, late sunlight reached down from street level through a grate further along. Ivanov turned off his LEDs too. The comparatively bright, green underground world became a darker, muted place again, but the night-vision goggles quickly adapted.

Ivanov could hear street noises close overhead. A truck rumbling through, and the crunch of hobnail boots stomping along a street in unison. A patrol of the People's Polizia, most likely.

The OSS operative took a moment to call up a mental map of the street above them. Albergo Grimaldi, the hotel where his contact, Anya, was staying, was less than two minutes' walk from the church where they had established an observation point, but many hours crawling and wriggling through these dark, constricted spaces. And it had not been the best observation point. A difficult angle in the turn of the street gave them only an impeded view of the *albergo*'s top two floors, but it was the best they could do. Approaching the hotel from below, unfortunately, entailed a much longer and more arduous journey; one that had just deposited them, reeking of filth, another minute's walk from their objective.

"Come," said Franco, taking a knife from his boot. "Our time is good. His woman will be waiting for us in the laundry block at the rear of the building."

Ivanov followed him, careful not to splash through the sewage. As they moved quietly along the drain toward the shafts of light created by the bars of the grate, he took up his own weapon – a silenced contemporary-era MP5. A bit on the heavy side due to the lack of composites, but the OSS Field Operations shop had produced a credibly effective copy. He was happy to have it.

Franco whistled through the grate. Ivanov heard the rumbling of steel-shod wheels and, a moment later, a fishmonger parked his cart overhead and reached down to lift the heavy metal grille for them. The smell of brine and fish gone too long without ice drifted down on them. With a quiet word of thanks, Furedi and Ivanov climbed up and squeezed through into the street.

It was deserted, save for their nameless helper, who nodded briefly, holding the bill of an old fisherman's cap, before taking himself off down the narrow, cobblestoned conduit. Moving swiftly, they reached the rear of the laundry. Franco, with his knife palmed for immediate use, opened the door and led the Russian past a group of women working through steaming piles of white sheets. As they moved, the women grunted and wrinkled their noses in disgust yet said nothing. It was as though the men were not there. An older woman, bent over and swaddled in black rags, hobbled after them with a bucket and mop. She set to cleaning the sewage they tracked behind them.

Franco looked around, concern on his face.

"What is it?" Ivanov asked.

"I'm not sure."

A woman screamed and the first shots barked out at exactly the same moment. The washerwomen screamed too, all of them scattering for cover and squawking like startled birds. Ivanov snapped out the stock of his weapon and flicked off the safety.

The doors to the laundry block crashed open to reveal two NKVD operatives in cheap Russian suits. Their eyes scanned the room, quickly falling on the two men, rank with excrement and filth, standing in the middle of a mountain of white linen.

Ivanov jerked the MP5 up to his shoulder and squeezed off a burst that caught the man to the left in the chest, dropping him in a bloody mess onto a basket of pillowcases. The other operative, a taller, shaven-headed man, dived to the floor, protected by a knot of screaming women blocking Ivanov's line of sight. The laundry workers stampeded for the door as he and Franco knocked them out of the way, searching for a clear shot.

A pistol roared and bullets ricocheted off the tile near Ivanov's ankles. The security man unloaded his clip from down low, near a table at the back of the room. Franco circled around a mound of linen, now stained with blood spray, and fell upon him as the hammer of the hapless Russian's weapon clicked on an empty chamber. The mafioso stabbed his knife deep into the man's throat and ripped it out through the trachea.

Taking his cue, Ivanov ran over to the door leading to the hotel and attempted to peer inside – only to have to pull back when the doorframe splintered from a fusillade of incoming rounds. Changing mags, he quickly emptied three 30-round clips into the hallway, chasing them with a pair of grenades. The entire room shook when they detonated.

Franco ran up to grab him. Ivanov brushed him off. "GO!"

03

South Rome (Allied sector)

At first, the owner of Osteria del Gallo insisted on clearing the best table in the house for them, but Harry refused to displace the family already sitting there. Aldo, the owner, then tried to convince the prince and his 'beautiful lady' companion to take his private dining room, in the restaurant's converted cellar, a space more suited to hosting two-dozen people. Harry's security detail thought that a spiffing idea, but he and Julia elected instead to sit at a small table in a secluded corner of the establishment. He also discreetly arranged to cover the bill of the poor locals who'd almost been kicked out onto the street on his behalf, part-way through their *insalata caprese*.

The del Gallo was a new place, a few blocks south of his apartment on Via Giustiniani. It was hugely popular with the Anglophone diplomatic crowd and those locals who could afford the top-tier prices. Harry recognized the MI6 station chief at a nearby table, sharing bruschetta and a bottle of soave with his opposite number from the OSS. Their protection details were even more obvious than his. At least, the first layer of protection was apparent: the bodyguards sipping water at the table next to the spy chiefs', and four more prowling the streets outside. There would be other, unseen lines of defense surrounding them.

The great game was played hard and fast here under the shadow of the Roman Wall.

"So, did you come to Rome just to enjoy your new status as an action-movie hero, or are you actually doing any work here?" Julia asked, as she tore small pieces from a ciabatta loaf to dip them into the bowl of olive oil and balsamic. "At the trade talks maybe – earning a little ambassadorial scratch on the side?"

"I suppose that depends on whether my girlfriend is asking," Harry replied. "Or whether Julia Duffy, ace reporter, wants to know."

She popped a piece of crusty bread into her mouth and sucked the oil from her fingers. "Girlfriend now, is it? Last week *The Times* referred to me as your 'long-time on-and-off companion'. I think that was some subeditor's idea of drollery."

"How so?"

She cocked an eyebrow before quoting an old schoolboy rhyme: "'She offered her honor, he honored her offer, and all night long it was on her and off her.'"

"Cheeky fuckers," he snorted. "New York or London?"

"*New York Times*, of course. Your *Times* can hardly bring itself to admit we're even dating." She paused long enough for it to become significant. "We are dating, aren't we?"

Harry leaned forward. "I thought we were fuck buddies," he said quietly, with a brief, mock-malicious grin. "That's how you describe us to Walter Winchell, that fucking toad."

Julia shrugged as she tore another small piece of bread from her roll. "He's a tool. But I knew he couldn't print it, or repeat it on the air. I just wanted to see his piggy little eyes spinning round. And you didn't answer my question, *Your Highness.* Business or pleasure? I do have a stake in your answer, so don't make me put my reporter's hat on. They still wear them here, you know – real hats with a press ticket in the band, and everything."

The head waiter arrived with two glasses of prosecco, rescuing Harry for the moment.

"I believe we are ready to order," he said, pointedly ignoring Duffy's question.

"Excellent, excellent," the waiter replied, lifting himself up on tippy-toe each time. "And Your Highness, and your lady friend, you will be having ...?"

Julia forcefully injected herself into the exchange while checking her old Apple flexiPad in a battered leather carry case. "We'll be having less of the patriarchal horseshit, while sharing the truffled mushroom, and the salad with arugula and pear and gorgonzola, and I'll be having the veal. With lemon."

"But of course, of course," the man said quickly, unsettled by her lack of eye contact and aggressive manner. Julia's fingers continued to glide across the surface, manipulating icons with taps and rubs, generating a multiplex stream of messages from around the world. Harry hadn't been able to eke a single bar of wifi out of his Ultima, so he assumed she was piggybacking on the local cell-net.

He put away the mad grin that wanted to break out and run wild all over his face. He knew all about Julia's issues with old-school gender roles, but in his experience, 1950s Italy wasn't that much different from what he recalled of its twenty-first century descendent. He wondered whether Duffy had spent much time in Rome before the Transition, smacking Italian men upside the head for being so presumptuous as to call her "*bella*".

"That all sounds bloody marvellous," he conceded. "We'll go with that, except I'll have the pig's knuckle instead of the veal. We'll settle on wine after the bubbles."

Their waiter retreated, keeping an eye on Duffy as he withdrew, possibly relieved to get away from the table with his testicles attached. It had been more than ten years since the uptimers had arrived in this world, and in places like California, London and Sydney, where they had settled after the war, their strange ways were now largely accepted. Indeed, much of the cultural and political baggage they brought with them – particularly their odd and unsettling ideas about women and race and sexuality and other identity issues – had been taken up by enough of the temps that it was sometimes difficult, at least initially, to pick a genuine uptimer from a contemporary who'd completely bought into the future and its promises. Harry was reminded of Julia's two colleagues earlier in the day. They would have been children when Kolhammer's fleet emerged from the wormhole on top of the US Pacific Fleet heading to Midway back in '42; yet from the look of them, you would never have known they hadn't stepped out of their own wormhole from the future. Not unless you knew what to look for. He did, and it made him wonder just how weird and off target the twenty-first century of this world was going to be when they finally got there.

It was rare for Harry to find himself contemplating uptime these days. Temporal theory had been taken out of the hands of science fiction writers and placed in the care of well-funded faculties at universities like Berkeley and Oxford. The currently accepted consensus was that the future he had come from still existed. But so did the alternate future that Dr. Manning Pope had created on board the *Nagoya* by exiling them all here. And an infinite number of other futures as well.

That was why Harry, along with most sensible people, had stopped bothering to worry about such things. There was no point, unless you were Albert Einstein or Stephen J. Hawking – who was still only eleven years old and studying with the great physicist in California, while receiving gene therapy for the motor neuron disease that had not yet manifested itself within his tiny frame.

Yes, best not to bother oneself with the infinite fucking Rubik's Cube of chance and probability that the Transition has brought into the world. Or this one, anyway.

He took a long swallow from the prosecco, which he enjoyed as much as he ever had any drink back up in the twenty-first. Possibly more so. Life here was easier for Harry Windsor than it had been at home. Even something as simple as a date with Duffy – and they were definitely dating – involved much less farting around and unpleasantness with the press than he had ever managed with Pippa back up when.

Julia tapped her iFlex and fixed Harry with a stare. "Still waiting."

"Sorry ... Misspent youth. It catches up with a fellow, you know. I killed a lot of brain cells in my twenties."

"We all did. But come on, really. You invited me to Rome. Is this going to be it for us – a quick dinner and a shag – or is there any chance you'll get away from whatever villainy you're up to this week? I don't believe for a moment you're only here for that ridiculous film or the trade talks."

The waiter returned with a plate on which sat a single large mushroom, steaming, lightly sheened with oil, garnished with shreds of deep green flat-leaf parsley, and smelling strongly of truffles. He sliced it in half before leaving them to their entrée. The restaurant was full now, the buzzing crowd split evenly between locals and foreigners, mostly Americans and Brits, just like them. One cheeky bastard strolled in talking loudly into a bakelite receiver which was tethered to a leather satchel at his side.

At last, the Ugly American has arrived, Harry thought. You simply can't do a restaurant scene in Rome without one. A waiter approached and pointed to the sign on the wall, displayed prominently in several languages, which implored guests to refrain from the use of wireless telephony.? "Now you listen here, Shorty ..." the American began.

Harry tuned him out without a thought.

"The General Agreement on Tariffs and Trade is hardly villainy," Harry said. "It'd have to be a shitload more interesting to qualify as that ... And I am actually doing my bit for the film," he added, almost apologetically. "It's a big deal for Pinewood, and expected to pull in some decent quids for them, and the tax man after he takes his considerable cut. But you guess right – I have a full dance card at GATT. Mostly as a glorified greeter for the embassy. Half-a-dozen wretched fucking cocktail parties and dinners where I get to tell a few war stories, listen to lots more, and do whatever Her Majesty my young grandmother's government asks of me to justify my rather generous income from the civil list." He paused for a second. "I'm afraid I have one on later tonight, in fact."

Duffy ignored the admission that they wouldn't be seeing each other later. "Regimental pay not good enough for you?" she asked as she carved off a small wedge of soft, perfectly braised mushroom. "Lost it all on fast women and slow horses?"

"Something like that," said Harry. "But I'm staying on for a couple of days after the gabfest wraps up. I thought we might take a drive down to the Amalfi coast, have a few days down there? Presumptuous of me, I know, but I presume you can get away?"

Julia waved off any problems with an airy flick of one hand. The candlelight in the restaurant sparkled and flared in a couple of bejeweled rings, but it was the scars on the back of her hand that stood out. And the calluses on her knuckles and palm. They looked a lot like Harry's scars.

She no longer worked as an embedded combat reporter. They didn't have them here, and even if they did, Julia Duffy would not have needed to work. She had invested wisely after the Transition and was now a very wealthy woman. The few freelance commissions she took on these days, she did for her own amusement and interest. Her scars, like Harry's own, she had collected on battlefields long past, and off in the long-lost future.

"Pfft," she scoffed, finally putting away her flex-iPad.. "Presume away. I only came out here to catch up with you. It's been a while, Harry."

Julia spoke these last words with just a hint of reproach. But he knew her well enough to understand that much of that reproach was meant for her alone.

"I'd love to get away for a couple of days with you," she continued. "I sometimes find ... I don't know ... Do you ever find yourself getting tired of them?"

She let her eyes wander around the room. He assumed she meant the temps. And yes, he did get tired of them. Of their whole world, in fact.

"Those girls I was working with this afternoon – and they really were girls in so many ways, not women. I'm mentoring them. That's what happens when you get a bit long in the tooth to do anything really awesome for yourself anymore. You teach others to be awesome. It's how I fight the good fight these days. Anyway, they're great girls, and tough as nuts, even though they got a bit giggly around you. The smaller one with the dark hair, Jessica, reminds me a lot of Roseanna. They both mean well, and they're like total zealots and converts to the cause, so they're never going to grief you with any of that tiresome bullshit the temps still go on with."

She sighed.

"But sometimes I just want to run away back to 2021. Or 2034, or whatever it is there now. Can you even imagine what it's like anymore. Back in the *real* modern world. It'd be great to just hang out with people who don't make every fucking minute of the day such a fucking effort."

"I have my rights!" the loud American with the phone-bag cried out as the waiter attempted to shoo him out.

Harry dabbed at his lips with a napkin. He had finished his half of the mushroom and pushed his plate away from him a little.

"It sounds like you really need to get to the beach," he said, nodding at her handheld. "Maybe unplug for a bit. Go primitive."

Julia rolled her eyes. "I thought we did that when we arrived here. But, you're right. I do. So yes, let's do that. I was going to file a few travel pieces while I was here – write the whole trip off for tax purposes, on general principles. But you know what? I think I might just take a couple of days to be a tourist again. I can wait for you."

Another waiter arrived to clear their plates, while a third approached with a wine list under his arm. Harry quickly negotiated a bottle of pinot grigio that everyone agreed would suit both of their mains before shooing away all of the attendants. Life as a standby royal, and later as an army officer, had at least polished up his attendant-shooing chops.

"That sounds like an excellent idea, Jules. Fucking smashing idea actually," he declared. "I wish I could do the same and just swan off this week. But I'm stuck here doing my party-princess routine while GATT's still on. They've left me a couple of hours free at lunch two days from now. Would you like to catch up then?"

Before she could answer, a frown furrowed her eyebrows. Harry looked back over his shoulder to whatever had caught her eye and found the senior of his two bodyguards approaching with a note in his hand. More interestingly, the OSS and MI6 chiefs had taken their own bakelite 'walkey' phones from briefcases below the table.

Bodyguards closed in around them and the waiter was strongly dissuaded from intervening.

04

North Rome (Soviet sector)

They made the relative safety of the sewer tunnels a bare minute ahead of their pursuers. Ivanov judged there to be at least a platoon of NKVD paramilitaries coming after them. The storm troopers forced an entry into the sewer system by the crude but effective method of blowing up a drainage grate.

"Move!" he'd yelled at Franco when he heard the satchel charges thud and clang on the iron bars.

His guide needed no prompting. He was already heading around the nearest bend, splashing up great fantails of foul-smelling black water and scattering rats before him. Ivanov followed, his ears ringing as gunfire crashed out, cutting off the sound of a woman's screams.

What just happened?

He had been tasked to contact a Russian man, Sobeskaia – a factory owner of some sort, someone important enough to be in town for the GATT conference – and to establish his bona fides as an ongoing source. Was the whole meeting a ruse? They were supposed to make first contact with this man Sobeskaia's mistress, at the back of the hotel where the couple were staying. Had it been a trap?

Possibly not, since the NKVD had sprung it *before* he arrived. Perhaps something had gone wrong at their end too. As Ivanov fled headlong into the darkness of the buried levels of eternal Rome, he did not much care. What mattered now was getting the hell out.

He powered up his NVGs, using infrared this time, and at once he could see that Furedi had done so too. Nor had the Italian needed to be told not to use the LLAMPS setting. If they stayed at this level, with some light filtering down from above, the heat signatures of the men chasing them would stand out starkly.

He heard shouts and the thudding of boots dropping into the drain behind them as Franco steered them around another bend, gesturing furiously for Ivanov to follow. He gave the impression of a man who knew where he was headed. That was good, because Ivanov had no fucking idea. The angry discordance of voices soon resolved itself into the harsh, stentorian barking of one man. A voice Ivanov recognized immediately.

Skarov.

The shock was almost great enough to stop him in his tracks, but the crack of a single pistol shot, followed by Skarov's curse, and two more shots immediately afterwards pushed him on. Ivanov bet that somebody had disobeyed an order to hold fire, and the NKVD spy catcher had summarily executed him.

He bit down on a curse as his head bumped and grazed the rough brick ceiling of the drainage pipe. Stars bloomed behind his eyes and a stinging pain told him he'd opened up his scalp. It would need disinfecting. The passage narrowed around them. Franco was already bent over double in front of him. To keep up, the much larger Russian man was forced to crouch low and duck-walk as quickly as he could. He concentrated on making as little noise as possible, on not stomping on the wet bricks as he hurried along, but rather in pushing himself forward like an ice skater accelerating across a frozen lake. A couple of body lengths up ahead, Franco passed through the underground world like a deeper shadow on the darkness, leaving no trace at all. His field craft was exceptional, thought Ivanov. For a petty criminal, he would have made a good special forces scout.

This way, the Roman gestured, before diving into a pipe that opened into a larger conduit. Ivanov followed the slightly blurred, cherry-colored figure without hesitation. The shouting behind them had died down, but not because Skarov and his men had given up. They were listening and waiting.

The pipe was slimy and smelled awful in a way that was slightly different from the usual miasma of the sewers. Even with the night-vision goggles, visibility contracted to almost nothing. Ivanov could feel the passage narrowing around his shoulders, but he forced himself forward anyway, trusting in Furedi to get them away. He could feel soft, obscene shapes and lumps of organic matter under his hands, but there was no way of telling what they were. They weren't retracing the path they'd taken to the hotel.

A barked command to give themselves up reached out from somewhere behind, but it was not followed by shots or the sudden flooding brilliance of spotlights.

He forced himself forward by inches.

The crawl through this section was long enough that Ivanov had time to ponder the presence of his old nemesis behind him. Better that than to dwell on the increasingly cramped and claustrophobic surroundings.

Alexi Skarov it was who had driven him from the Rodina, where whole armies of soldiers and spies had proven themselves unable to lay hands on Pavel Ivanov during the late 1940s. As he ghosted through the heart of Stalin's vast charnel house, Ivanov had lit the fires of half-a-dozen Chechnyas and Georgias. He had inflamed the murderous passions of jihadists, separatists and insurgents, along with mere criminals and gang lords. With these efforts he piled up a mountain of corpses and bled out whole divisions of the Red Army, spreading death and chaos from the occupied wastelands of Japan, through Siberia, down into Afghanistan and even once within the walls of the Kremlin itself.

He had so infuriated Lavrenty Beria that the poison dwarf had offered not just a huge monetary reward for his capture, but the precious freedom of real choice to any man who delivered Ivanov before him. Millions of roubles hung like the sword of Damocles above his head, but also the prospect of freedom to anyone who betrayed him. Deliver Pavel Ivanov into the hands of the NKVD, promised Beria, and not a finger would be raised against you should you wish to take your reward and leave for the so-called 'free world'.

It was quite a compliment, in a way. He had really pissed them off.

But material reward was not Skarov's motivation. The demon in the tunnels behind Ivanov now was much more dangerous than any bounty hunter or freedom seeker. Alexandr Dmitry Skarov was Stalin's executioner-in-chief. He hunted Ivanov not for money or freedom, but because for him it was the right thing to do. Skarov was a true believer in the revolution. And Ivanov knew from bitter experience that he would spill oceans of blood to prove that belief and to secure the people from the mistakes of any false history revealed by the Transition. Or the Emergence, as it was generally known on this side of the Atlantic. To Stalin, to Skarov, to millions of other believers, the arrival of the uptimers, the way they had torn the settled order of events into bloody shreds, was proof positive that the forces of history revealed by the dialectic were undeniable. The revolution could not fail, and so it had not. Time had wrenched itself apart to set things right.

They were fucking crazy, Ivanov knew. But crazy dangerous.

A giggle slipped from his lips, which he stiffled into a snort. It was possible, Ivanov admitted in the quiet moments of rare solitude, that he might well be a little bit insane himself. Just possibly.

He shook it off.

Skarov had hunted him without relent, killing Vendulka and the rest of his original team one by one over the years until Ivanov was all that was left. He recruited others – there were always others and Ivanov knew what to promise them, even if the words rang increasingly hollow. They died as well, and Skarov had driven him from Russia, and then from all her conquests. Nowadays, Ivanov was only able to snipe at the Communists from the edges of their continental gulag, darting in and out of cities like Rome, which lay on the border with the free world. And now here

Skarov was, on the very borders of the evil empire, reaching out into the free world to try to lay hands on him again.

Strange that he had lasted this long. He'd expected to die in Siberia with his Cossack allies years ago. If he were a religious man, he might've believed there was some sort of plan. But there wasn't, he had decided long ago. There was only chaos, and the mission.

The tightly constricted crawl-space conjured up images of Skarov embracing him and squeezing and squeezing until the last breath was gone from his body. Just as Ivanov feared he would not be able to squeeze through, he felt Franco's hands grip his shoulders with the strength of iron claws, pulling him forward until he popped out of the confined space like a cork. Tumbling down a curved slope of old worn cobblestones, he fetched up in a puddle of decomposing meat and vegetable matter. He had lost track of time and had no idea how long he'd been crawling through the pipe.

"We are below the markets here," Franco said in a low voice. For an instant, Ivanov latched on to the hope that they had somehow passed beneath the Wall and into the NATO-controlled part of the city. Or at least underneath it. But Furedi quickly killed that hope.

"Not the People's Market. *My* people's market." The mafia scout was grinning, as though he had just told one of the funnier jokes Ivanov should expect to hear in his life.

Ah, thought the Russian, *a black market*. An actual undeclared marketplace, where food and medicine and other goods smuggled in from the free south by the Trimbole family could be sold for massive profits, or sometimes simply distributed to secure the loyalty of those whose hunger the Family had eased. There was a reason the OSS preferred to work through operators like Franco and his kind on this side of the Wall. This was their world and their people. They were always going to be the A-Team here. The Soviet security barrier ran east to west, along Via Aurelia, skirting north of the Vatican, cleaving the city in half and winding out past Villa Borgese (now the Italian Communist Party HQ), before punching right through the war-scarred ruins of Nomentana district and turning north along the great ring road that would have circled the city. Now it defined the edges of Stalin's prison camp in the south; creating a dark mirror image of Berlin's fate in the original time line. Northern Rome was a small island of tyranny, an outpost for Stalin and Beria a few miles south of the greater border between free Europe and their empire. The city Wall was not yet complete. Some sections were massive gray battlements, some were simply killing grounds of razor wire, minefields and free-fire zones. But it was effectively impenetrable to all except the likes of Ivanov and his guides. There was no going over the Wall, but you could still go under it.

Looking around, Ivanov found himself in a stone chamber no bigger than a child's bedroom. Steel grates barred three gaping holes underfoot. They looked like ancient wells, with iron bars rather than surrounding walls to prevent anyone falling in. His eyes watered with the stench of rotting food. It was difficult, with the combat goggles set to infrared, to pick out individual items from the septic sludge under the tread of his boots. But here and there he could see a lettuce leaf hanging limp over an iron bar, crushed eggshells, or the splintered bones of what looked like a haunch of meat, maybe lamb or goat. Looking upwards, Ivanov discerned the outline of what appeared to be two large steel plates just above them, close enough to reach out and touch.

"A storeroom up there," explained Franco. "We smuggle supplies in there, and other places. We give the people a good price. Good for us and good for them. Good enough that they look after us. Especially now. Come."

Ivanov followed him to a set of steel rungs buried in the rock face. They climbed quickly. Franco used his shoulders at the top of the improvised stepladder to force open a heavy wooden shutter. Ivanov had not seen it in the gloom. They crawled up and out into a room that was obviously above ground. Windows, opaque with dust, admitted the last dying filaments of daylight. He flipped up his NVGs, disoriented by the fact they had been underground most of the day. It had not seemed that long when they were being chased, and yet, at other times, the minutes had dragged by with glacial slowness. The Russian could smell faint traces of coffee, cured meat and cheese, but the room was as bare as the abandoned church in which they had holed up earlier. Franco secured the wooden cellar door with a thick iron latch. It had obviously been left open for him, and Ivanov began to wonder at just how much pre-op planning La Cosa Nostra had done for what was supposed to be a simple contract job. An escort mission.

"Follow quickly now, Russian," said Furedi as he hurried over to a set of heavy double doors that opened out on an alley. "Your friends will not be far behind."

The temptation to assure Furedi that they were not his friends was strong, but Ivanov held his tongue. His fate was now almost completely in the hands of this gaunt-looking stranger with iron-gray hair.

Franco tapped on a metal pipe by the main doors, a coded sequence of some sort, and Ivanov shook his head as he recognized a ship's speaking tube. Franco lifted the hinged metal cap at the end of the tube and blew into it as if he were playing a trumpet. Listening with the intensity of a safecracker, he had an answer in a few short, harsh words in the local language. An argument of sorts ensued, but it seemed that Ivanov's guide had the better of it, given his satisfied nod when he flipped down the cap again.

"We wait. Not long. They send help."

Ivanov said nothing, taking the opportunity to re-arm himself from his small equipment stachel, a precaution that Franco was happy to follow. The Italian took out a handgun and fixed a suppressor. As the mission principal, Ivanov enjoyed the privilege of carrying the big artillery. He had chosen an MP5K-PDW over the more commonly used re-engineered Uzis preferred by other operatives. Heavy firepower in a tight, compact package; a simple fold of the stock had made his passage through the Roman underground much easier and more secure.

Pausing for a moment to clear away any filth and muck that might interfere with his weapon's operation, he covered the tunnel they'd just exited with the suppressed muzzle, prepared to provide a proper welcome to any interlopers. Tweaked by the OSS Field Operations shop for the reliability normally found in an AK-47, Ivanov's weapon could generate a cyclic rate of fire of 800-plus rounds per minute, easily emptying the drum mag's 100 rounds in less than twenty seconds. With a muzzle velocity of 375 meters per second, anyone who attempted to follow them would walk into a wall of copper-jacketed hollow points.

"Nice gun," Franco commented. "My *capo* has two just like it."

"I do not doubt that," Ivanov said quietly.

They stood in silence for another five minutes, listening for the approach of Furedi's allies, who would presumably appear from the street. And listening even more intently for the NKVD to come bursting up from below.

A soft knock at the door – another coded cadence by the sound of it – and Franco admitted two men dressed in dark, threadbare civilian suits. The light was fading fast, but Ivanov could still make them out as middle-aged, with sunken cheeks, and eyes with all the light burned from them.

It didn't feel like a set-up, but Ivanov was careful to keep all three grouped within a tight firing arc. For their part, they did nothing to arouse suspicion, such as separating and approaching him from different directions. Still, he kept the safety thumbed off while the Italians conducted an urgent council of war in low, hurried tones.

"It is settled. We go back now," Franco announced when they were done.

"To do what?" Ivanov asked. He was willing to defer to this man's judgment in matters of navigation, especially under fire, but picking a fight with the NKVD, and with Skarov in particular, was getting into the realm of strategic decisions that were well beyond the guide's responsibility.

"To kill them," replied one of the new arrivals. He was the slightly older of the two, Ivanov thought; a little taller, somewhat sturdier too. He didn't have quite the harrowed and hungry look of Franco and the junior man. As Ivanov's eyes adjusted to the deepening gloom he could tell this one looked well fed and well used to being obeyed.

"I am all for the killing of NKVD," said Ivanov. "It is what I live for. But you will not live for long if you go back down there now looking for a fight."

The three Romans exchanged a guarded look as though they thought themselves in the presence of a dangerous fool.

"Perhaps," said the man he now took to be their leader. "But we agreed to help you because you were sent to us as a man who has killed many Communists. This is good. You have brought more Communists for us to kill. Also good. They are below our feet right now – we are watching them. So let us do what you were sent to do. Let us kill them all."

A gloomy darkness pooled around them as Ivanov tried to reason with the mafioso.

"Today I did not come here to kill Communists," he began. "And you know that. Today I came to talk to a woman called Anya, the woman of an important Party man, to learn something from him. That did not happen, and I don't know why. I don't know whether he is alive or dead, but that man remains the reason I came under the Wall."

"*We* are the reason you came under the Wall," said the mafioso. "We gave you Franco because our friends the Americans told us it would help to kill more Communists. You cannot speak to this man you were looking for now. But that does not matter. Provenance has set another goal before us. We must go now into the old city again. Below. While we still know where they are. Do not fret, Russian," the man added, nodding at the trapdoor, "we will not blunder into them. There are many paths back down. This is our city. Not theirs. They have already blundered by coming here."

Ivanov held up his hand. "All right. We will go back down. But there is a man down there, a Communist called Skarov ..."

"We know of him," said the leader, almost dismissively. "A man with many sins to answer for. Perhaps today he will answer for them."

"Perhaps," Ivanov conceded. "But first he needs to answer to me. Killing a handful of Beria's snakes means nothing if you do not clean out the viper's nest. If I can get to Skarov, find out from him what happened to the man I was supposed to meet, I might learn something that will bring us all much closer to the day we can kill or drive away all of the Communists. Not just the few down in the sewer below us."

The other man's face was becoming lost in the gloom. His eyes, already dark and sunken, seemed to disappear as the last of the light faded away.

"All right then," he said. "I can make no promises about what will happen. Only the good Lord can know that. But we will try to preserve the life of this Skarov so that he might make his confessions to you."

The man's strange choice of words and his demeanor gave Ivanov pause. There was something about this man, something familiar, he thought. He was no mere killer. He seemed more than that. And then Ivanov caught the resemblance as Franco turned slightly to listen to the street outside.

He was much older than the young man in the SIS files. Time had not been kind to him. (But then time had not been kind to any of them.)

It was Marius Furedi. The priest.

05

North Rome (Soviet sector)

Occupied Rome often suffered from brownouts and occasional full-blown power failures in the early evening, when demand peaked. The few streetlamps that ran off the city grid in this part of Rome flickered and died as the infiltrators emerged from the secret warehouse. Light spilling from the open windows of apartments overlooking the alleyway died at the same time. Ivanov wasn't sure whether this happened by mere chance or the design of his companions. He was grateful for the cover, whatever the case.

Franco introduced his companions as Marius and Giorgio. The Russian had no doubt that Marius and Franco were siblings. Nor that the elder brother was the padre of which Franco had spoken. Marius had none of the coarseness or bravado of a mid-level gangster about him. His English was more fluent, more sophisticated, than Franco's, and when he spoke even briefly, he betrayed the cultured intelligence of a man who had been trained by an academic order. Perhaps the Jesuits. They were very active beyond the Wall.

He wore no clerical garb about him, but twice Ivanov saw him reach for a non-existent rosary or scapula about his neck. Franco and Giorgio, on the other hand, gave the impression of men who had spent their entire adult lives in the lower orders of a criminal organization. Their banter was softly spoken and sparse, but littered with the crude argot and curses of the Roman street. It made sense that the Furedis should work together, he supposed. No bond was closer than blood. But an operational connection between the mafia and the Church? That would bear thinking about later – presuming there was a later.

The four men were exposed to the street for only half a minute, as they hurried from the black-market warehouse to a rundown *pensione* across and a little ways up the alley. Ivanov and Franco returned their weapons to the satchels they carried, but the small, fast-moving procession – two dark-suited men and two in disgusting, soiled coveralls – would surely draw the attention of any patrols or informants.

Yet the street was deserted. The windows, balconies and doors of the apartment buildings overlooking them remained empty. Had Ivanov been leading a platoon of troops down this narrow, deserted alley, his skin would have prickled with the sense of something wrong, of a threat gathering just beyond the edge of perception. But here he felt ... cloaked. As though the city itself had deliberately looked away from them, choosing not to see what was in plain sight.

This was probably one of those neighborhoods where Russian troops and the People's Polizia trod quickly and lightly, and mostly around the margins. He would not have been surprised to discover that many of the bodies of the occupiers and collaborators that turned up in the river had breathed their last here.

Hurrying into the *pensione*, they passed by an old man smoking a hand-rolled cigarette who paid them no more attention than he did the scrawny black, one-eyed cat mewling and circling around his boots, looking for food. He didn't even wrinkle his nose at the stench of their filthy coveralls. It was as though they were not there.

Marius led them down a narrow corridor, smelling of boiled tomatoes and burned garlic. They passed through two apartments that appeared to have been turned into one by amateurs with sledgehammers. A hatchway under a flight of stairs led down to another flight, taking them back underground. Ivanov reached for his night-vision goggles, but Marius stayed his hand. The Russian heard a match strike, and half a second later it flared into light. The priest – not that he had identified himself as such – touched it to a candle. The taper took the flame and the mellow golden light bathed the men. Ivanov was careful not to look directly at it, trying to preserve at least some of his night vision.

They were back underground again, in some sort of storeroom. Wooden shelving lined the walls of a long narrow chamber, close enough that Ivanov could not stretch both arms out. Glass jars and terracotta pots appeared to fill most of the shelf space, with tinned food and bags of rice, stamped A GIFT FROM THE PEOPLE OF THE USA, stacked near the entrance.

"This way," said Marius, who had armed himself with his brother's weapon. Silencer and all. Franco was now carrying an old British Sten gun. Unsilenced. Giorgio had procured a shotgun from somewhere, all of them tooling up as they made their way down here in darkness.

Ivanov retrieved his own weapon, the MP5, from his bag. He had to reattach the suppressor, since the submachine gun would not fit in the knapsack with it screwed on. As a precaution, he also fetched out and fitted his NVGs, although he didn't turn them on, keeping the lenses flipped up.

"From here on we must be quiet," Marius said. "As quiet as the grave – unless you wish to find your grave today, Russian."

Ivanov replied with a flat stare. For the moment he felt numb; a dangerous place where his temper had been known to slip in the past.

The elder Furedi was unaware of Ivanov's state of mind. He gestured for them to follow. The four men crept down between the long lines of preserves and American food aid, stacked high on both sides of them. The far end did not culminate in a rock wall, as it had first appeared in the dark, but in old gray woolen blankets, hung over an exit that had been carved into the bedrock of the city perhaps 1000 years ago, perhaps more.

As he had been doing for most of the day, Ivanov crouched low to avoid hitting his head on the roof. He had cleaned out his scalp wound and applied a salve but didn't bother with bandages since they wouldn't adhere to his sweat-soaked, dirty scalp. Still, he did not care to reopen the wound before heading down into the sewers again. Assuming that's where they were headed. There was no telling underground. He might spend the next hour belly-crawling through a drainage pipe, or creeping across the roofline of a long-buried village.

Marius led them deeper into a series of tunnels that seemed to have been carved out of the city's foundations for the very purpose of concealed movement. It was possible, even likely, that Marius knew of these tunnels because they remained in the collective memory of his mother church. The early Christians were, at times literally, an underground movement.

It seemed they walked, and occasionally crawled, for nearly half an hour. At first, Ivanov wondered how these Romans could possibly know where Skarov and his men were anymore. The NKVD would not have given up the chase, and might well have poured more searchers into the hunt. But there wasn't the slightest chance that Skarov would have remained in the chamber close to the hotel laundry, where he had first forced his entry into the underground world.

That small mystery resolved itself soon enough, when Marius stopped a few minutes into the journey to speak into another voice tube, exactly like the one Franco had used back in the warehouse. Clearly, the Furedis were receiving updates on the Russians' whereabouts from allies elsewhere in the tunnel system. Alerted to the presence of the speaking tube, Ivanov began to see them sprouting from the wall at seemingly random intervals. Minutes might go by without encountering one, and then two or three would appear at the juncture of a couple of tunnels. The priest and his bandit companions appeared to be intimately familiar with the layout of the ancient passageways and their crudely effective communication system. Ivanov wondered when it had been installed. Obviously not when the tunnels were dug.

The fetid stink of the sewers and drains was not nearly as powerful down here. Not initially, anyway. When his nostrils flared and his nose twitched at the first strong whiff of raw effluent, Ivanov wondered if they might be approaching their destination. The candle Marius was using to light their way had burned down about half its length. Their pace slowed and eventually he brought them to a halt where the tunnel widened slightly before splitting into two diverging passages. He motioned for the others to gather closely around him.

He spoke in a voice so low, Ivanov was forced to lean forward to make out each word. "We will separate here. Franco, you will take the Russian to the upper gallery. Giorgio and I will join Stefan and Marco on the southern terrace."

The last two names meant nothing to Ivanov, but he assumed these were the men Marius had consulted. Were there more of them around? Did they work for the priest, and for his masters in the Vatican? Or were they from Franco's "other" family. He hoped the latter. If they were about to do battle with an NKVD strike team, he preferred to have killers and thugs on his side rather than ecclesiastical agents. Although, for all Ivanov's certainty that Marius Furedi was a soldier of God, the man had about him the cold, detached air of a soldier who had seen enough death to become fatalistic about his own chances.

"Franco will lead you, Russian," said the priest. "Follow him and do as he says. The Communists have reinforcements. We have counted fifteen of them in the chamber ahead and more on the way."

He must have seen the look on Ivanov's face.

"It matters not," he assured the Russian. "We shall kill them all."

"But not Skarov," warned Ivanov.

"No. He is not there."

The numbness disappeared, replaced with a low, boiling cauldron of emotion. Ivanov let some of the tension loose from his left hand before squeezing it into a fist, so tightly that knuckles popped. So now they were off on a forlorn hunt to bag a few foot soldiers for no apparent end.

"Do not concern yourself with him," said the warrior priest. "He has returned to the surface. We are watching him, and we will take up our business with him when we are done here. If you want your foe, you must draw him back down. And making a sacrifice of his men will do just that."

Fury and murder burned behind Ivanov's eyes, but he had not survived so long in this game by allowing himself to vent his feelings uncontrollably. More than ever he was beholden to these Italians. Not just to guide him through the world beneath the streets of the city, but to guide him back toward his original objective – the contact at the Grimaldi. And now also to Skarov, who seemed to be using Sobeskaia as bait. Ivanov diverted his anger and used it to clear his mind, burning away fear, extraneous thoughts and any desire he had to slit the throats of his Roman companions. With a deep breath, he clamped down on ill-feeling and turned his wits to the task at hand.

"It is for the best," Marius told him. Franco nodded solemnly beside him, at least having the good grace to look a little ashamed. Giorgio remained as he always had – a stonefaced killer.

Marius blew out the candle and Ivanov reached instinctively for his NVGs. Still set to infrared, they picked out the heat signatures of the three Italians but little of the background detail. The men appeared like three red ghosts floating in the vacuum of space. Switching to low light amplification was a surprise. The tunnels were more brightly illuminated than he would have imagined when the priest extinguished the candle. A hot wash of photons was leaking from a powerful light source nearby.

The Furedis and Giorgio moved off without apparent difficulty. Franco trailed his fingertips along the ceiling and the roughhewn rock face of the ancient shaft. The other two disappeared before Ivanov could see whether they were negotiating their way in the same fashion. For the moment, he decided he would stick with LLAMPS vision, adjusting the photon gain as they drew closer to the light.

The tunnel took a sharp turn to the left and climbed steeply up a flight of worn steps carved directly out of the granite floor. A millennium or more of foot traffic had smoothed the edge of the steps and eroded a deep bow in each of them. Franco was moving very quietly now, reminding Ivanov of an old and mangy but dangerous cat. He drew to a stop a few paces beyond the top step.

Another man awaited them there.

Or rather, a boy, to judge by his prominent cheekbones and the fiery eruption of acne that covered most of his face. His eyes shone brightly in the NVGs, like poisonous green stars, making him a monstrous visage that was not helped by his vulpine smile. Precisely the sort of creature who might live in the underworld, with greasy matted hair and a mouthful of crooked teeth.

The boy gestured at Franco, who turned and pointed at Ivanov's combat goggles, indicating that he should remove them. The OSS operative did so, surprised to discover that after a few seconds of squeezing his eyes closed to adjust, he could see quite well. He could also hear the voices of a number of NKVD troops somewhere below their position.

Franco had led him into a cavern just large enough to accommodate the three of them. To Ivanov's dismay, the boy was armed with a Great War vintage bolt-action rifle. There was no time to change that now.

A careful peak around the entrance of their cave confirmed that the troopers had gathered in a much larger cavern beneath their vantage point, and were all toting re-engineered AKM-74s with folding stocks and rails loaded with LED tactical lights, laser sights and, in some cases, grenade launchers. They were also illuminated by battery-powered camp lights and appeared to be setting up a base from which to conduct a systematic search. Ivanov closed his eyes and did his best to recall every detail of the site picture he had snapped in his mind.

He saw three camp lights, a stack of bedding, two fold-out tables covered in rolls of paper – drawings and maps of the sewers (from the city engineers perhaps?), a couple of modular-frame tents, and even a portable cooking stove. There were at least twelve to fifteen men down there, similar to the report Marius had received.

What Ivanov did not see was any sign of Skarov, of course. The spy catcher had run where the trail was hot. Back to the hotel, as Furedi had said, to secure the only link to Ivanov that he had. The *boyar*.

The former Spetsnaz officer shook his head, unhappy with the way this was playing out, with him being pushed across the chessboard as somebody else's pawn. He was used to moving other people around – not being played by them. Resolving to speak to the priest before this whole thing went completely off the rails, he had just moved toward Franco, intending to whisper that he urgently needed to see his brother, when a Russian voice shouted out in alarm. Within a second, two explosions roared and shook the ground underfoot, knocking Ivanov slightly off balance.

The boy snarled as his rifle began cracking out single shots, then Franco's shotgun boomed, and the whole world went up in a roar of gunfire and a string of grenade explosions. Ivanov cursed, once, in Russian, and swung the muzzle of his submachine gun around the mouth of the small cave. He fired controlled, short bursts at first from his MP5 in the general direction of where he remembered small knots of NKVD troopers had been standing, less than a minute before. The suppressor did its job, deadening the muzzle flash and the report of his weapon, but making him feel slightly ridiculous in the devastating uproar of pitched battle that had erupted all around them.

Bullets hummed and whizzed past, stitching the rocks, bricks and concrete around his position. An explosion far to his right blew out a chunk of the ceiling, probably from a grenade launcher.

Ivanov gave up on short bursts and emptied the 100-round drum in a general arc from left to right. Expended in a few seconds, he dropped the drum and replaced it with a conventional magazine. Repeating the process three times, Ivanov sprayed the bulk of his ammunition into the cavern below, before throwing a grenade down into the fray.

The boy grunted and gurgled as his throat exploded, painting Ivanov's face with a splash of hot gore. His body dropped and rolled over the lip of the cave mouth, tumbling away into the firestorm below. Franco racked shell after shell into his shotgun, raining hundreds of pellets down on the Russians, never once speaking, even to curse, while he did so.

An enormous explosion, seemingly volcanic in the confined space, stabbed Ivanov's eardrums like hot knitting needles. The blast was far too large for a hand grenade; after a moment's disorientation, he surmised that one of the gas cylinders attached to the camp stove had ruptured and exploded. The volume of fire trailed off immediately.

Dark shapes emerged from the far side of the large cavern. Marius's men. They drew sharp blades and knelt down next to the Russians who still cried for their mothers, gagging on their own foamy blood. They slit throats, stabbed through carotids and into hearts in much the same workmanlike fashion one might go about strangling a chicken for dinner.

"We go now – hurry!" said Franco. Ivanov could barely hear him over the ringing in his ears. They dived back into the tunnel system, navigating by the light of fires burning behind them.

This is bullshit, he thought, before realizing that he had spoken or perhaps even shouted aloud. Furedi ignored him, charging forward, navigating as he had earlier, by running his fingers along the walls and the rock face above his head. When the flickering orange light of burning equipment and bodies was no longer sufficient, Ivanov slipped his NVGs back on, before swapping out a magazine from his weapon.

Unsurprisingly, Marius and Giorgio were waiting for them at the junction of the two tunnels. The priest – if that was indeed what he was – seemed entirely unperturbed by the action. He accepted the death of the boy with a quick nod of his head and the sign of the cross.

"This will bring many more of the Communists," he said. "They are already in the tunnels and catacombs."

Ivanov could not help himself. "A brilliant plan then, Padre. Kill a few stupid troopers so that we can get ourselves killed by many more."

Giorgio's lips peeled back from his teeth like a dog, but neither Franco nor Marius reacted. Nor did the elder Furedi demur at being addressed as "Padre".

"It all serves a purpose," he replied calmly. "God's purpose and yours. The man you seek, this businessman, he is no longer guarded by one hundred of Stalin's attack dogs. Only a small squad remain."

Ivanov looked at him as though he were a particularly stupid child.

"Because they are all down here hunting for us."

"Exactly," said Marius. "You can offer your payer of thanks later."

06

South Rome (Allied sector)

"Oh dear," said Harry. "I hope we've set a place at table for Mr. Cockup, then."

The Secret Intelligence Service chief was unimpressed with his attempt at levity. *These people*, thought Harry, *no appreciation for the classics.*

"This is serious, Colonel Windsor," Carstairs said, conspicuously declining to address him as "Your Highness". "Sobeskaia is running hot, right now, and you are the only person he'll agree to run to."

The three men – Harry, Talbot Carstairs and Stan Walker, Carstairs' OSS counterpart in Rome – all stood around a small conference table in the secure room at the British Embassy. "The Quiet Room", as Harry thought of it, although he would never have used that phrasing in present company. The local spymasters both played to type. Carstairs, with his shiny, bald head and round, almost babyish features, was every inch a civil service man, even if his service was performed in secret. Walker was old-school OSS, a veteran of the mad, bad days of Wild Bill Donovan. The sort of brute who was most happy blowing things up and hurting people. Probably too smart for one of the military intelligence workshops, and too dumb for the Ivy League think tank of the CIA which, in this world, did not dirty its hands or bloody its knuckles with anything as gauche as direct action.

The SIS station chief ran a hand over the shining dome of his head, almost as if he were brushing hair out of his eyes. It was most probably an old habit, Harry thought.

"Gentlemen, we simply do not have the time," said Carstairs. He tapped two fingers on a buff-colored manila folder lying on the table in front of them, leaving a couple of faint, greasy fingerprints behind, just beneath the only words printed on the cover.

VALENTIN SOBESKAIA.

Harry's stomach growled. Apart from a few mouthfuls of truffled mushroom, he had not eaten since the morning. The glass of prosecco with Julia hardly counted, and he now deeply regretted waving away the finger food at Sir Alec's movie premiere. He shook his head as frustration got the better of him. Jules had been understanding at the restaurant, but then, she was more than familiar with the demands of last-minute, unexpected deadlines. Still, he felt awful for having dragged her all the way to Rome, only to abandon her almost immediately. Nothing about this meeting suggested he'd be able to catch up with her again anytime soon either.

"All right," he sighed. "Valentin Sobeskaia. I suppose you'd better tell me all about my new best friend."

The OSS man threw a quick glance at the locked door. More a nervous twitch than a conscious attempt to reassure himself that they could not be overheard.

First though, to Harry's surprise and not inconsiderable annoyance, Carstairs insisted on the formalities. Opening the file, he began to read from a card pasted to the inside, carefully sticking to the exact wording.

"*Colonel Windsor, you are about to be briefed into a Top Secret Ultra file. By accepting this briefing, you agree to be bound by the provisions of the Official Secrets Act of—*"

"Oh come on, I don't think this—"

But Carstairs cut him off, holding up one hand like a traffic policeman. Meanwhile he continued his read-through, explaining to the prince and 25-year military veteran the full range of penalties that would apply to him (yes, even him) under the *Official Secrets Act 1939*, were he to divulge the contents of this file to any unauthorized person or persons.

Unable to keep his annoyance in check, Harry wordlessly implored Walker to intervene. The American just grinned back at him, like a hammerhead shark. He was obviously used to the bureaucratic obsessions of his colleague.

"Sign please," Carstairs said in conclusion. He passed Harry a fountain pen and indicated where he needed to add his signature to the shortlist of people who had been given access to the file.

Harry scrawled out his name, adding an *HRH* for good measure, and stabbing the pen into the paper to emphasize his disgruntlement. He couldn't believe he was stuck in this small, airless room in the basement of the embassy. Not when he could be finishing his dinner date and making plans for a couple of days of wanton carousing on the Amalfi coast.

"Sure you wouldn't like that in triplicate, old boy?"

Carstairs appeared to consider the offer seriously, while flipping open the file and leaning forward to spread its contents out across the table. He had a small splotch of pasta sauce on his collar. "Signing once is more than enough to get you in trouble," he replied. It was the only time that Harry had ever heard him attempt a joke. Or what he assumed was a joke.

"Now, Valentin Sobeskaia," the spy chief began, in the practiced cadence of a man repeating a briefing he had given many times before, "one of Stalin's pet commercial *boyars* ..." He looked up at Harry to make sure he understood the meaning of the term. Harry waved him away.

There was nothing particularly exciting or even classified about the information. For all that the Soviets had unleashed an army of theoreticians to explain the failure of their revolution in Harry's time, and for all that the resulting explanation was utter bullshit, the Kremlin had paid at least some heed to future history. They would never admit it, of course, but they'd attempted to learn from the success of their Chinese comrades in freeing up some market controls, while maintaining an iron grip in the political realm. Sobeskaia was a beneficiary of that complicated two-step. A Party boss who had been authorized to run a state enterprise along commercial lines. He was one of millions of Soviet citizens who had profited directly from Stalin's own, very particular version of *perestroika.*

"Sobeskaia acquitted himself well, first as the senior foreman and then as director of a tractor factory given over to tank production in the early days of the war," explained Carstairs. "He then disappeared from view for at least eight years, but reappeared in good health as one of the first authorized managers of a corporatized State Business Enterprise."

"A toaster factory, if you can believe it," said Walker, with a short barking laugh. "Automatic toasters. And they worked too, the son of a bitch! He was building them before we were. Exporting the suckers all over the goddamned world."

Harry was beginning to get a feel for where this might be going. He stretched his back, which felt cramped. Closing his eyes against the glare of the overhead fluorescents, he decided to hazard a guess.

"We're assuming, I suppose, that Comrade Sobeskaia spent those eight years covering himself in glory with the NKVD's Functional Projects Bureau."

"Ha!" Walker chimed in. "As the philosophers say, if a bear shits in the woods but nobody smells it, it was probably working for Lavrenty Beria."

"Philosophers say that?"

"The ones from the faculty of mixed fucking metaphors do, yeah."

Carstairs handed over a couple of photographs of the state-approved businessman. They were good quality, which didn't surprise Harry at all. Although the Iron Curtain had trapped hundreds of millions of people inside Stalin's gargantuan prison camp, for those with the trust of the state, travel was much easier than it had been in the original timeline. Over 1000 "enterprise *boyars*" – businessmen and women who, like Valentin Sobeskaia, ran corporatized operations for mother Russia – were now in Rome for the GATT conference. Many of them were even staying on this side of the Wall, doing business, signing contracts, making money with their ideological nemeses in the free world. Just as the once and future Chinese Communists would have done.

The photographs Harry flipped through all looked as though they'd been shot while Sobeskaia was visiting the West. Taken from a variety of angles and distances, they mostly featured backdrops of expensive restaurants and hotel lobbies.

"Was this bloke staying in Free Rome?" he asked.

"No," said Carstairs. "He was ensconced at the hotel Grimaldi in the Soviet sector. But he had a get out of jail free pass to cross through the checkpoints. He was supposed to be there today. In his hotel."

"So why the flap over a toaster salesman gone missing?" asked Harry.

"Well, his fucking toasters are kicking the ass out of GE," said Walker, not altogether facetiously. "It's not like he has to pay top dollar for his slave labor, you know. Asshole's moving into electronics next, transistors and maybe even silicon, according to the word here in Rome."

"But that's not why you want him, is it?" Harry asked, perusing the rest of the documents laid out before him, which amounted to a particularly meager report, he thought. Mostly just base-level commercial intelligence about the operations of Prozpekt Elektric, the state corporation run by Sobeskaia. Harry shook his head. Cartairs had made him sign the Official Secrets form to read a bunch of newspaper ads for some of Prozpekt's cheap consumer wares. A couple of washing machines, a microwave oven, and a steam iron. All of them looking as though their designs had been stolen from sources uptime – which, of course, they had. The Sovs hadn't just gained access to 21C military technology after the Emergence. They'd also grabbed up a treasure trove of data on eight decades worth of development in consumer goods and, Harry thought wryly, a history lesson from Deng Xiaoping in how to get the West to pay you to bury them.

"No, we have little interest in Comrade Sobeskaia's cheap microwave ovens and toasters," Carstairs replied. "I don't care for these so-called 'microwaves', personally. Unlike Mr. Walker. I find they either burn one's food or leave it frozen in the middle, or both."

An exchange, unspoken but unmissable, passed between the station chiefs. An in-joke or an old disagreement, perhaps. Carstairs moved on, retrieving a small plain envelope from the back of the file, which he opened before tipping the contents out onto the table.

"Sobeskaia smuggled these to us via an intermediary."

"His dame," added Walker.

Harry frowned at the metal shavings, scattered over an advert for a Nijinsky coffee machine clipped from *The Telegraph*. The tightly curled metallic tendrils were a dirty silver color and quite lustrous under the harsh white fluorescent light.

"Well, I'm guessing it's not radioactive," Harry said, only half joking. "You do know not to play with plutonium, don't you, Mr. Carstairs?"

"It's tungsten," replied the British spymaster. "Chinese tungsten, mined in the mainland Communist territories, of course."

"Of course. I don't suppose Prozpekt is branching out into jewelry or exotic yacht keels, then?"

"What?" That threw Carstairs, if only momentarily.

"Niche uses," the prince explained. "Not nearly as popular as using it for armaments."

The other men nodded. Walker spoke then. "You got it. Penetrator rounds, supersonic shrapnel – all the good stuff. You don't need tungsten for it, but unless you have a whole heap of depleted uranium lying around, it's not a bad option."

Harry picked up one of the small metal shavings. It felt dense and hard, and he was careful not to pinch it too firmly in case he cut himself.

"So, what's the story? You're sure Sobeskaia isn't launching a weaponized toaster onto the market?"

"Could be," Walker conceded, to Carstairs' obvious chagrin. "Well, we don't know, do we?" the American added in reply to a glare from his SIS counterpart.

"No, we do not," said Carstairs. "We don't know much about Mr. Sobeskaia at all. Other than that he chose to reach out and make contact with us via an informal channel, requesting a meeting while he was here in Rome for the GATT conference. He sent us these shavings as a teaser."

"Spiffing. So I suppose your people talked to his people?"

"Tried to," said Walker.

"And at this point Mr. Cockup joined the party, right?"

Carstairs flushed bright red, the skin on his neck nearly matching the color of the pasta sauce on his collar. "The OSS put one of their best men on it," he said ruefully.

"One of *our* best men, Talbot," corrected Walker. "He was a shared asset."

"I do note your unfortunate use of the past tense," said Harry.

Talbot Carstairs swept up the small pile of tungsten shavings, carefully placing them back in the envelope.

"A shared asset, yes, yes," he conceded. "One of your people, actually, Colonel."

"Sorry? You mean from the 22nd SAS, or another uptimer?"

Carstairs nodded at the last option. "Ivanov, the Russian. You know of him, I assume? One of your special commando johnnies."

"We've met," said Harry. "A long time ago now. Just after the war."

He searched his memories of the encounter. Ivanov, as he recalled, was looking for SAS men, either uptime or contemporary, to freelance inside the USSR. Harry had sent him off with nothing but his best wishes.

"Well, he was supposed to meet Sobeskaia this evening, over in the Soviet sector," Carstairs went on. "At the Albergo Grimaldi, where Sobeskaia was staying. But it's all gone rather pear-shaped, I'm afraid. We don't know anything about what's happened to Ivanov, other than that there's been some gunplay out there."

"And bombs going off," added Walker as he took up the explanation. "We put him together with one of our local contacts. A guy who could get him over the Wall and back."

"Mafia," said Harry. It wasn't a question.

"They love their freedom and their country as much as the next guy," said Walker. "Anyway, Ivanov was just supposed to meet with Sobeskaia. Shake him down for some information, see what was up with this shit ..." He waved a hand toward the small envelope in front of Carstairs.

"But the meet-up went wrong," surmised Harry.

"Never even happened. This Sobeskaia asshole sent his girlfriend, the broad who got the shavings to us – who we're pretty sure is dead now, or as good as. He's fucking her, so he trusts her. They're looking to get out from behind the Wall. Figured they could buy a ticket with an ounce or two of shredded tungsten.

"Anyway, we've got no real-time link to Ivanov. His presence there is deniable. But we got other sources over in the Soviet sector telling us there's been a heap of gunfire, some grenades going off, all of it in the vicinity of the Grimaldi. Sovs are saying it's just fire-works. But the word on Sobeskaia's girlfriend is good, we reckon. He sent her to the meet as a decoy. Probably knew it was a fucking washout."

"Charming. And Sobeskaia?"

At this, Carstairs appeared to be trying to suck the fillings out of his back teeth, while Walker merely grimaced. The SIS man spoke first.

"He's turned up here in South Rome, at the same cocktail party you're due to attend this evening. He arrived about forty minutes ago, although it seems he's been over in our sector for a day already. We now suspect that the rotter never intended to meet with Ivanov. He sent his mistress into a trap while he hid out here and then ran for it, turning up at our shindig tonight. Uninvited. Unexpected, of course. But he *is* a senior member of the Soviet trade delegation, so he gained access. He has been hanging off the arm of the consul ever since, demanding to meet with you. Naturally, the caterers are going spare, because now the party's absolutely swarming with security men. Ours, theirs, and God only knows who else."

Harry rubbed his eyes, which were throbbing with the start of a headache.

"I don't suppose he said why?"

"To defect. To you. Personally."

Harry nodded slowly as he made an effort to control the adrenaline surge. He felt dizzy with hunger, and perhaps even a little giddy from the drink earlier. Not the best of shape to find oneself in at the current impasse.

"And I imagine there's some reason why you haven't just walked him out the door and into a car?"

Walker smiled. "Yeah. It's like Talbot says. About ten minutes after Sobeskaia showed up at Babington's, an NKVD snatch team arrived. All of them with bona-fide invites. Junior trade envoys, second assistant cultural attachés – that sort of crap. And all of them now circling our guy like fucking bull sharks. I think that's why he wants you in there, Harry. You're a two-for-one deal: an SAS officer and, now and forever, an heir to the throne. He figures they won't dare throw down on him while you're standing there. And if they do, what the hell – you're just the sort of guy who'll jump in and take a bullet for him."

"The hell I will," Harry retorted. "And I'm no more an heir to the throne now than you. *And* I haven't even had dinner yet."

Carstairs shook his shiny bald head. "I'm sure, Colonel Windsor," he said, "that just like the gossip rags who follow your every move, Mr. Sobeskaia is either unaware of or unimpressed by the Succession Act of 1949 and subsequent amendments. As far as he is concerned, you are an heir to the British throne, here and in the future. He wants to defect to you, and only to you. As for dinner, we all missed out, but you can eat when you get there. I hear the shrimp cocktail is excellent."

Talbot Carstairs smiled weakly. His second attempt at wit for the evening.

Never a good sign.

07

North Rome (Soviet sector)

After an hour of crawling, running, waiting and crawling some more, Pavel Ivanov found himself back in the narrow, subterranean storeroom. He recognized none of the tunnels or crawl-spaces through which Franco had just led them, but when they pushed through the heavy gray blankets there was no mistaking the shelves piled high with terracotta jars and bottled preserves.

He'd kept his own counsel following the short battle with the NKVD, preferring to have out his issues with the priest when they were not fleeing pursuit. But even now the opportunity wouldn't arise. Once out of the underground labyrinth, the Furedi siblings exchanged a few whispered words before Marius made the sign of the cross over his brother and disappeared back through the blankets and into the tunnels. Franco grabbed Ivanov by the elbow and drew him upstairs.

"You must move now, Russian."

Biting back a curse, he followed, stowing his MP5K. They hurried up the stairs, returning to the maze of cramped corridors that seemed to run through a couple of apartment buildings that had been linked by dint of smashing through adjoining walls. Nobody paid them any notice in the dreary gloom. Not the old

men he saw smoking hand-rolled cigarettes and playing cards on a front stoop in the dark of evening. Not
the mamas and nonnas who met at the junction of two
well-trafficked hallways to exchange limp bundles of
green vegetables under a single, flickering low watt
bulb. Not the children who raced up and down, lost in
some game involving laughter and mock gunplay and
squealed Russian curses.

In some ways, he thought, the war, the Transition,
the Communist occupation, the wrenching destruction of the twentieth century's settled history – none
of it had much affected the day-to-day life of Franco
Furedi's people. The mafia soldier had probably passed
through here dozens of times in the past twenty years
covered in filth and blood. And never once did anyone
see anything. He wondered how long their hard-bit-
ten *omertà* would last under interrogation by the
People's Commissariat for Internal Affairs – the
NKVD. Men and women who would remain obdur-
ately silent while they themselves were being tortured
often became babbling torrents of information by the
time you had snipped the second or third finger from
their child's hand. In Ivanov's personal experience,
and to his unutterable shame, he knew that in especially masculine societies like this one you could move
the whole process along with greater speed by taking the tiny manhood from a captive's favoured son.
(Or even just the tip, if you were a soft-hearted type,
like him.) It always made for terrible reprisals later on,
though.

When he was thoroughly lost, in both reality and
memory, Franco surprised him by turning off the
ground-level passageway and heading up a staircase.

They passed by open doors through which the Russian caught glimpses of family life in this ancient slum. Small rooms crowded with many children and old people, but very few men of working age. He smelled tomatoes cooking and onions being fried, scents strong enough to overwhelm the mold and rot and the rank barnyard odor of unwashed, tightly compressed humanity. There was little sign of the future forcing its way into this place. Even the cheap, crudely made consumer goods that had lately been pouring out of the Soviet slave factories into the West were nowhere in evidence.

After some more twists and turns, Franco put a finger to his lips, signaling for Ivanov to be quiet, as he pushed through a closed door on the top floor of a tenement that looked like it had been occupied by Rome's poorest workers since da Vinci was a boy. There were fewer people up here, Ivanov realized. In fact, they hadn't seen anyone on the stairs or moving about the hallway for the last few minutes. He followed Furedi into the gloom of a tiny apartment, which was empty save for a couple of thin, stained mattresses and the detritus of what looked like US Meals Ready to Eat. The former Spetsnaz officer recognized the signs of a lay-up point. He also recognized the voice tube system as soon as Franco used it to talk to yet another hidden accomplice.

Curiosity, bordering on compulsion, tried to draw Ivanov over to the one grimy window, to see if he might establish their location, but training and experience kept him rooted to his spot in the dark, just inside the door. He was still beholden to his guide to lead him to safety.

"*Sì, lo sarà*," the Italian said quietly before closing the cap on the speaking tube. He then gestured for Ivanov to follow him cautiously to the window, where they took up positions on either side.

"Look, but be careful," said Franco, jutting his chin out in the direction of the street. The old lace curtain was faded and rotting, allowing Ivanov to put one eye up to a moth-eaten hole, rather than having to twitch the fabric aside.

He was surprised to find they had a view overlooking the hotel where he was supposed to have met his contact. Sobeskaia, the businessman. The narrow street outside was blocked by an ambulance, an eight-wheeled BTR-60 armored car, and three long black sedans – prewar Mercedes, by the look of them, a favorite of the NKVD for the fear they inspired. The Gestapo had often arrived in the middle of the night in exactly these models.

The ancient cobblestoned thoroughfare was a strange, contrary space, with the expensively renovated hotel sitting between two run-down, and boarded up apartment blocks. They had almost certainly been seized by the state to create a buffer around the accommodations for the Party boyars. Up and down the street, run-down blocks with crumbling stucco faced off against newer, brutalist architecture, rammed into the spaces created by street fighting during the first, chaotic weeks of Soviet occupation. It reminded Ivanov of other cities where rich and poor, the powerful and impotent were all crammed in tightly, contending to see who would end up controlling the streets.

As he watched, medics carried a body out of the hotel on a stretcher. The corpse was covered in a bloodstained sheet. "Our man?" he asked simply.

"No," said Franco. "Probably his mistress. Killed by your Skarov, according to our people in the *albergo*. We do not know what happened to this Sobeskaia. But we are looking for him. We will find him."

Ivanov felt himself adrift on a dark sea. Who the fuck were these people of Furedi's in the hotel? He wondered whether his OSS controllers on the other side of the Wall knew what had happened yet ... The Russian had no way of contacting them while he was in the field. This was a deniable operation, after all. His long history of freelance action against Moscow would lend credibility to the inevitable protests that he was a rogue actor, should he be caught. God knows, there were enough of them among the 10,000 up-timers marooned here a decade ago. But Ivanov also knew that Rome seethed with spies, and it was unlikely that he would have been let loose without hidden overwatch of some sort. Overwatch probably had no idea where Sobeskaia was either, but they would already know the mission was a washout.

Not for the first time, Ivanov had to swallow his frustration at the primitive methods of his contemporary allies. For all the great leaps in technology since the Transition, in many ways he was no better equipped than an agent smuggled into Berlin or Prague in the original Cold War.

Franco waved one hand down at the street, where Ivanov could see a few sturdy old couples taking their evening stroll in defiance of the occupiers' best efforts to intimidate them. Even here, under the boot of the Communists, people tried to wriggle free at least once every day, dressing in whatever old, shabby finery they may yet possess to walk their local streets, to greet neighbors and friends, and wherever possible to dine and drink and talk. If they were lucky, they might even push back the unpleasant realities of life behind the Wall, just enough to sleep a little easier that night.

He envied them.

For Pavel Ivanov, when he closed his eyes at the end of the day, only dreams of death and horror waited. He would sometimes wake, biting back on a strangled cry, rubbing at the scar that ran down his right temple. It was an old wound, but full of phantom pains that haunted him between sleep and wakefulness.

His fingertips probed gently at the scar now. It was throbbing. Playing Russian roulette with a Makarov had seemed like a bright idea at the time. A beacon of reason, in fact, that had shined with unusual brightness in a very dark moment, many years ago. A shitty round had saved his life, but left him scarred. Ever since, he had turned away from the solace of vodka and misery and focused on the mission.

As he watched and rubbed at his wound, children ran about below. Perhaps the very ones they had passed earlier. They certainly seemed to be playing the same game.

"We will find Sobeskaia," Franco repeated. "Everyone looks for him now."

Resentment and rage warred within Ivanov, and he struggled to maintain his detachment. The mission was a scrub. It had been blown somehow, and now Skarov, his oldest surviving nemesis, was scouring the city for him. Or at least the portion of it known as North Rome. It was time to accept defeat and tactically withdraw.

He was about to step back from the window when he saw Beria's chief spy catcher emerge from the hotel. The sight of the tall, shaven-headed NKVD killer brought forth a galvanic, almost visceral response. He was a powerfully built man, like Ivanov, but high cheekbones and sunken eyes gave him a cadaverous look and accounted for his nickname within their closed and dangerous world: the Skull.

At the sight of his death's-head visage, rage flared like hot flames, washing away Ivanov's impatience and unhappiness with the way this operation had gone. Rage, intemperate and hard-favored, threatened to blind him, as he stood there at the window in the gloom of the evening.

Skarov, dressed in black from his expensive, hand-stitched steel-capped shoes, to the knee-length leather coat that swirled about him like a cape. Skarov his nemesis – just a trigger-pull away. He was a family man when not on duty; a dedicated father who played with his two boys and only daughter, who never strayed from his wife of eighteen years. However, as a Guardian of the Correct Future, Colonel-General Alexi Skarov's duties often took him away from home and hearth, leaving his family to tend to themselves. Ivanov still had the souvenir from a visit, to the Skarov dacha nearly two years after Vendulka had met her end at his hands.

As his eyes remained fixed on the Skull, he fondled the souvenir, which he kept in a small pouch hung around his neck. Yes, he knew very well where to cut a man like Skarov. Ivanov felt the giddy urge to laugh again. He coughed and clamped it down.

"Come, we must go," said Franco. He tugged firmly at Ivanov's elbow.

But the Russian would not move. He stood as though rooted to the floor, axes in his eyes, staring at the Skull. He could feel his very organs seething and slithering over each other inside him.

The coat. That long black atrocity. He had worn it as a provocation. He had worn it because he knew they would be meeting somewhere today.

Ivanov could not take his eyes off the coat, sewn together from the tanned hides flayed from his closest comrades. Vennie. Hamilton. Kicji.

A grave provocation, he thought, fingering the soft leather pouch at his neck again. Dying would not be hard if it meant stripping that obscene coat from Skarov's corpse. *I could die content tonight, if only I could take Skarov with me.*

Ivanov had to clench his fists to stop himself reaching into his weapons satchel and retrieving the submachine gun. He was too far away. As cathartic as it would've been to empty a whole magazine down into the street, the chances of killing or even hitting Skarov from this distance were not good. Not without killing a number of innocents. The bastard probably wore a ballistic vest in any case.

"*Now ...*"

The Roman dug a thumb into his elbow joint, pulling Ivanov out of his dark reverie with a spike of electric pain that ran up his arm and into his shoulder.

"We must go *now*. More of them are coming."

As he spoke, two heavy trucks, Ural-375 troop movers, lumbered around the corner and slowly edged their way forward through the narrow confines of the ancient cobblestoned backstreet, to join the fleet of official vehicles outside the Albergo Grimaldi. The massive

six-wheeled trucks muscled their way past the pedes-
trians, wheels up on the paving stones of the footpath,
forcing the old men and women taking *passeggiatto* to
back themselves up against a wall or climb the front
steps of the nearest apartment building to avoid being
crushed. Even the swarms of children who had braved
slaps and occasional kicks from the uniformed NKVD
guards at the hotel, kept their distance from the trucks.
Every day someone in this city died under their wheels.

Franco dragged him away from the window before
the reinforcements jumped out of the rear. Someone
knocked at the door, softly, but following the mafia
man's lead, Ivanov did not reach for his weapon. The
door opened a crack and an old woman put her head
around carefully. She carried an oil lamp in one hand
and a large linen bag under her other arm. When she
saw them in the weak light she offered up the heavy
cloth bag, before retreating back out into the hallway.

"We change now," Franco ordered, stripping off his
once-gray municipal worker's uniform.

Ivanov followed his example, not bothering to
undo any buttons, just ripping the soiled coveralls
open and stepping out of them. Franco tossed him a
cold, wet hand towel, which he used to wipe off the
worst of the filth. They had no time to clean themselves properly, but that probably wouldn't matter.
With the power supply so unpredictable, and basic ne-
cessities like soap often hard to come by, the streets
of Occupied Rome were not the freshest-smelling avenues down which he had ever wandered. Ivanov did
take a moment, however, to properly clean the wound
to his scalp, rinsing it out with a stinging antiseptic
solution he took from his satchel.

They climbed into their new clothes as quickly as they could – although they weren't exactly "new", thought Ivanov, as he pulled on a pair of pants roughly patched together from stiff, paint-dappled canvas. One leg was shorter than the other. A thread-bare shirt lacked buttons, and sported apparently indelible sweat stains under the arms. The sleeves were so tight he feared to rip them if he flexed his hands. A once black jacket, gone dark gray with age, started to tear at the seams as he tried to get it over his massive shoulders. Even in the dim light he looked ridiculous.

"This will not do," he said, deciding the moment had come to take control of the operation. Furedi and his comrades had agreed to get him in and out, but they had also agreed to put him together with Sobeskaia. That wasn't going to happen now, and he had to question whether their exit plan was also shot.

Franco, who looked much more at home in his worn-out vagrant's apparel, took umbrage. "It is all these people have, Russian. The Communists strangle them. Food, clothing, medicine for the old people and the children, they have none of it ..."

"And I am grateful for the help. But this will not work. I will stand out in these clothes. Draw attention. We need another option."

"I told you, my people do not—"

Ivanov cut him off. "Your people have done enough," he said, adding, "I would not ask more of them" – lest the Roman take offense at his ingratitude. "But dressed like this, we're not going back down underground, are we?"

"Not far. Just a few streets away. Then we walk through the night markets. Communist markets – but they allow the farmers to sell produce there once a week. Very crowded, it will be good cover. And farm people," he said, backhanding the Russian in the chest, "they do not dress for church at the market."

Ivanov heard the tailgate of a truck drop down outside, and the shouts of NCOs ordering their men into the street. Risking a brief glimpse through the lace curtain, he was able to confirm that the troops were NKVD, not Red Army. He saw Skarov consult with a senior lieutenant, who mostly nodded and took orders from the civilian in the black leather coat. The officer soon had his men detailed into squads of four to search the buildings up and down the street.

He and Franco had five, maybe ten minutes before one of the squads stumbled across their lair.

"Okay, now we must leave," said Ivanov. "We go your way at first, but then we go mine."

***

They did not spend long underground this time, and they moved with much greater haste and almost no concern for stealth. The ground beneath them rumbled. Bursts of gunfire, shouts and sometimes screams, even the occasional crump of a grenade came as if from a great distance, amplified and distorted by the weird acoustics of the buried city. It sounded like construction work.

"Marius," explained Franco, as though the sounds of battle needed explaining.

The special forces veteran wondered how much of this clash would be reaching the ears of anyone listening on the other side of the Wall. Aside from the rumbling vibrations beneath the streets, perhaps none of it – or even if it did, no one would take notice. That appeared to be the Roman way.

Rome was a frontier city now. A great metropolis fated by a broken history to sit on the boundary between two empires. Like Berlin in his youth, like Budapest and Constantinople before them, like Tokyo now, Rome was a shadow factory. And the shadows had teeth and claws.

He and his guide avoided the fighting, hurrying through tunnels, some of which were simple root cellars and basements, avoiding the deeper passages where it seemed a great battle was being fought. A battle that few would know about, beyond those who survived it.

"Up, up now," said Franco as he pushed through an iron cage door and into the barrel room of a bar or tavern. The smell of wine gone sour was very strong, even though the subterranean space was mostly empty.

"Where are we?" Ivanov asked. He had decided the time was almost upon them when he would have to reassert control of this minor disaster.

"An old taverna," the other man said, pointing at the rough wooden beams just over their heads. "Closed by the Communists, but we still meet here sometimes."

"Of course." Ivanov was beginning to understand just how vast was the city hidden beneath the view of its occupiers. It wasn't just a matter of subterranean caves and tunnels. There was another Rome, a free Rome, hidden just under the surface of things in every street and alleyway above them.

"Explain to me, describe for me, exactly where we are going, and what I will find on the surface," the OSS operative said, standing his ground and halting Franco's progress toward the wooden staircase at the far end of the cellar.

The Italian frowned, impatient to keep moving, but he did as he was asked. "It is as I tell you, Russian. We are under the night markets for this district. These are the approved markets where farmers are allowed to sell what is left after the Communists have taken everything else."

Ivanov gestured for him to hurry on with his explanation. He was well aware of how the city government in the Soviet-controlled sector ran the marketplaces. Again, learning from the lessons of future history, the Kremlin had allowed its subjects some freedom. Not a lot, but enough to avoid the completely empty shelves that had done so much to undermine the rule of the Communists in Ivanov's own time.

"No, no," he said, shaking his head. "I need you to describe the tactical environment. How well lit. Is there CCTV? You know, cameras. How many stallholders, roughly? How crowded is the market? How many patrols? Are they on foot or is there a checkpoint, or a police station nearby? How many entrances and exits are there – where do they lead to?"

His guide understood now and nodded his head.

"What for do you need to know this, Russian?" Franco asked. "You have a plan, yes? I will need to know."

"I have an idea for a plan, but first I need to know what we are walking into."

The mafioso took a moment to think it through before kneeling down to draw a rough map of the small piazza above them. As he described the layout of the markets, and the usual ebb and flow of customers, all watched over by regular street patrols of the People's Polizia, Ivanov's idea for a plan began to take shape.

08

South Rome (Allied sector)

Nothing ever happens at a reasonable hour in this country, thought Harry. *What sort of cocktail party kicks off at nine in the evening, for God's sake?* Along with his empty stomach, it was a gripe that occupied the prince's mind as he fitted the fighting knife into the sheath strapped inside his left forearm. By 2100 hours, went Harry's reasoning, a civilized cocktail hour was over, and anyone with half a brain and a decent buzz on had already partnered up with some willing trollop and was back home, pants down, on the tool.

While Carstairs and Walker waited on him, he secured the stiletto blade and practiced drawing the knife a few times without opening an artery or slicing the sleeve of the dinner jacket they had supplied. He wasn't too concerned with Secret Service's wardrobe budget. It just wouldn't do to get the thing caught up on a cufflink, say, when he needed to be sticking a couple of inches of cold steel into some bolshie Ivan.

"It'll do, I suppose," Harry said, but he would've far preferred to kit himself out properly for a caper that was almost a laydown *misère* to go pear-shaped. Carstairs, however, adamantly refused to let him wear a shoulder holster, or indeed carry any sort of firearm into the party.

"We can't have you going off half cocked with some enormous cavalry pistol, Colonel Windsor. Lord, think of the diplomatic muddle."

Presumably the Foreign Office was up to arguing away the dire diplomatic consequences of him stabbing a "junior cultural attaché" from the NKVD, but not if he were to shoot the fellow over the punch-bowl. Well, there was always a lot of silverware lying around at these embassy piss-ups ... It wasn't beyond the realms of the possible, should things get a little sporty with Beria's men, that he could argue he'd just picked up the nearest shellfish fork and improvised a defense.

"I was rather thinking of the muddle that a bloody Makarov would make of me, actually," replied Harry, as he settled the cuff of his dinner jacket over the weapon.

"Ah fuggedabouddit. That's a damn fine-looking penguin suit and you wear it like a boss," Stan Walker drawled, borrowing a bit of arcane uptime slang that had already come into and out of fashion after the Transition. "Be a pity to ruin the cut of your jib with a big-ass hand cannon stickin' out for everyone to see."

Harry didn't bother arguing. The spy chiefs assured him that the floor would be crawling with about seven layers of security.

"No matter how many goons the Smedlovs send in disguised as junior cultural pussies," the OSS man repeated, "you won't be needing that pig sticker."

Harry had insisted on fitting the knife anyway, and thankfully they didn't object. His minders at Scotland Yard probably would have. In Harry's experience, Mr. Plod tended to take the business of guarding their 'ighnesses very seriously indeed, even though in this world there were no bearded nutters or IRA hooligans to cause trouble. The former simply hadn't evolved, at least not yet, and the latter had been forestalled in their murderous evolution by an accelerated political accommodation with Northern Ireland's Catholic majority. Harry was more likely to need guarding from Julia Duffy if he stood her up again.

His security detail, on the other hand, gave him no trouble. Carstairs had already seen them off, pulling rank when they'd all arrived at the embassy.

"Remember, Colonel," the SIS boss said now, as they left the Quiet Room and walked down two flights of stairs to the motor pool, "we're not sending you in there to crack on with your usual Lord Jim commando shenanigans. You are to walk Comrade Sobeskaia out of the front door, surrounded by my people, who will be responsible for any such shenanigans as are needed."

"A human shield, then?"

The uptime reference wasn't lost on the temps.

"Your own safety is as important as the Russian's," Carstairs intoned.

Harry didn't believe it for a second.

He left the diplomatic mission on his own, save for the driver who was more than a driver. They made for Babington's Tea Rooms on Piazza di Spagna, where the British trade mission was hosting drinks for Commonwealth and Naples Agreement member nations. The route took them through the diplomatic neighborhood, and along some of the finer shopping avenues. He kept a look out for Duffy, who would probably be salving her feelings with a retail binge.

He did wonder sometimes why she still worked, when she didn't really need to, but then he didn't really need to either, did he? He could live as a tick on the Civil List, making himself scarce while he swanned about the world's more obscurely exclusive playgrounds. But having tried that after the war Harry knew how quickly he grew bored.

He'd always been the type to grow dangerously bored, at least after he finished up his tours in Afghanistan and Iran.

He sighed, and let the lights and crowds become a blur as they motored toward the reception.

Babington's was a safe, if rather uninspired choice, in Harry's opinion. It was old enough to have attained institutional status amongst the city's English-speaking community, having survived both world wars and the chaos of occupation and division. The Cornish pasties and sausage rolls would come piping hot, the pastry crusts crisp and golden, and the scones with marmalade and the apple tea cakes would be perfect – but they'd all be served without a hint of irony. There'd be no playful rebooting of stodgy old, pre-Cool Britannia food styles tonight. He knew, from having suffered through a handful of these events already, that the embassy served up top-shelf stodge simply because the ambassador really liked top-shelf stodge.

Rome's traffic, as always, was hellacious, but it was even worse tonight because of the faffing around for GATT. Miles of bunting and flags hung everywhere. He noted the uniforms of at least five different NATO armies mixed in with the crowds that surged across roads and through intersections. Still, Harry's Rolls-

Royce glided through most of the snarls and traffic jams, escorted by four outriders, white-helmeted MPs on growling BMW motorcycles. To clear the way, an ASLAV-variant armored car traveled just ahead of them, flanked by its own Military Police escort. The locals, like all Italians, showed scant regard for the sanctity of traffic laws or the dignity of official convoys, but the water cannon atop of the ASLAV quickly cleared a path through any obstructions. Harry shook his head at least twice as they roared past crowds of drenched and angry bystanders shaking their fists at the official procession.

"Soak them to the balls, and their hearts and minds will follow," he muttered to himself as he weighed up the odds of actually getting to the Amalfi coast with his bird. Perhaps it wouldn't go pear-shaped. Perhaps he could do this job, get in and out, and even lay claim to taking an early mark and scarpering off to the beach before the end of the week.

The lights of a thousand shops and restaurants, all teeming with life, seemed to promise a brighter future. He knew it was, in part, an illusion created for GATT. The Allied administrators had whipped up a great deal of sponsorship money for a raft of cultural festivals to run at the same time as the trade talks. They were every bit as keen to craft a good impression as their communist counterparts on the other side of the Wall – although, of course, the Sovs were mostly interested in blocking unflattering views of their workers' paradise, rather than burying any faults under tinsel and glitter.

After nearly half an hour of stop-start driving they reached the restaurant, which sat to the left of the

Spanish Steps, climbing up from the piazza to the church of the Santissima Trinità dei Monti. The stairs, the widest in Europe, as he recalled from high school geography, were framed on the right by the nineteenth-century home of the poet John Keats. This, Harry supposed, accounted for the predictable choice of Babington's as a venue for the cocktail party. The Steps district had become something of a Little England in the last few years, after British forces had taken responsibility for this quarter of Free Rome. Revelers spilled out of the three faux English pubs within a beer bottle's throw of Babington's Tea Rooms. Dozens of Carabinieri formed a loose line between the footpath drinkers and the formally dressed guests heading into the cocktail party. That was an arrangement Harry could approve of. The city's police on this side of the Roman Wall were likely to exercise much looser control and apply a significantly lighter hand than their counterparts a short distance to the north. Some of these Italian rozzers, who looked magnificent in their pressed and colorful uniforms, were doing their utmost to chat up the hundreds of young English and American girls there on the fringes of the crowd.

The driver threaded Harry's Roller through half-a-dozen vehicles waiting to deliver their passengers to the embassy function. The Spanish Steps seethed with the crush of thousands of people enjoying the mild night and the small outdoor cinema, which tonight was showing *La Dolce Vita*, in front of the grand church. The Moonlight Movie festival was just one of many cultural asides to the vast economic conference that was GATT. A boon to the city, but a bugger of a thing when you needed to be anywhere in a hurry. The crowds were simply horrendous. Especially wherever uptime movies were being shown. Piazza Navona was impassable during the Harry Potter screenings.

The older, gnarlier, less wizardy Harry spotted the NKVD's inner-perimeter muscle as soon as the car slowed at the brightly lit drop-off point. Five slab-shouldered, stone-faced Slavic goons in gray, ill-fitting suits. All of them wore earpieces and stood like apes with arms akimbo – partly because their upper bodies were so overdeveloped courtesy of mandatory steroid regimens, and also because, to Harry's trained eye, they were wearing double-harness shoulder rigs. If these men were following standard NKVD procedure, each one would be packing a long-barreled GSh-18 for his dominant hand, and a Czech-inspired Škorpion vz. 61 machine pistol in the other holster, for less accur-ate and discriminating "clearance work". He felt like he was going up against a pack of weaponized gorillas with a letter opener hidden up his sleeve.

These dumb thugs weren't the real threat, however. They were here to draw his attention and that of the protective details supplied by Carstairs and Walker. They were bullet magnets. Salted throughout the happy, heaving crowd of civilians tonight, though, would be other men and women who, nondescript to the point of invisibility, would do nothing to draw attention to themselves. Even if that meant making utter arsehats of themselves to fit in. The helplessly drunk American girl in a Harvard sweatshirt throw-ing her arms around the nearest Italian police officer could be one of Lavrenty Beria's deep-cover wetwork specialists, or she could just be a pissed college student like the rest of them. You wouldn't know until the guns came out.

It was hopeless, utterly hopeless. He would gladly have given the whole fucking teddy bears' picnic a miss and walked the three miles to Julia's hotel. But duty called, as it always fucking did.

Harry stepped from the Rolls, smiled and waved to the small band of press photographers, using the opportunity to scan the crowd.

"Harry! Harry! We love your movie!"

He waved at the two young women, not nearly as drunk as the Harvard girl, but still a few sheets to the wind. A long time ago, in an alternate universe far, far away, he might have wandered over to make their acquaintance. Here he simply mouthed *Thank you* and gave them a thumbs-up before heading into the restaurant.

Babington's entrance was crowded. There appeared to be about eight guests, all of them formally dressed like him, held up at the security desk. Harry heard the first snatches of angry Russian as he reached the back of the small knot of pissed-off Smedlovs.

"This is intolerable," someone growled in heavily accented English. "We have invitations right here. I can see our names there, on your list ..."

Then Harry did a double take. No, not at the Russians piled up in front of two large airport-style metal detectors – they were almost certainly NKVD – but at David Gower, the former English cricket captain. Or unborn English cricket capt ... Whatever the actual fuck, he shook his head at the sight of a young man who, at first glance, was Gower's double. Perhaps an uncle or some more distant relative.

"Your Highness, so glad to see you – please step this way," said the young man, with the polished tones of an Oxford graduate, and the smooth, gliding walk redolent of another, more exclusive place of learning; the Secret Intelligence Service's close-combat finishing course at Albany Street barracks. Of slender build, with blue-green eyes, and curly blond hair cut somewhat longer than the regulation military length, he had the polished manners of a diplomat and the hard, calloused hands of someone who had spent years being trained to kill with them.

And this fellow did look remarkably like the left-handed batsman.

"Is there some problem here with our Russian friends?" asked Harry, shaking off his surprise and getting into character.

"Nothing for you to concern yourself with, Your Highness," his greeter assured him. "Just a little misunderstanding over the guest list."

The Smedlovs broke off from arguing with the two hard-faced door bitches (almost certainly Carstairs' people) who had refused them entry. As soon as they recognized the man they thought of as the heir to the British throne, the Russians turned their anger on him.

"Is this how your government demonstrates bonds of friendship and trust, sir?" said one, obviously the leader of the group. "We have been invited here tonight, then told invitations no good. This is deliberate insult to the Soviet peoples." At this, the man drew himself up and puffed out his chest.

"And which of the Soviet peoples are you?" Harry asked pleasantly.

"Viktor Kuryakin, second assistant secretary, Cultural Division. And you, as senior representative of Her Majesty's government, Prince Harry, must make these amends. Otherwise, there will be international incident."

Harry's eyes twinkled as he grinned and patted the Russian on the back – copping a feel of the butt of his handgun in its shoulder holster as he did so.

"Oh, I'm sure there'll be an incident, comrade," he said, before moving into the hallway and leaving them behind.

09

North Rome (Soviet sector)

The market square, lit in the sickly yellow glow of sodium bulbs, was small but crowded with busy huddles of stallholders, farmers in from the countryside, and women of various ages. All of this last group, despite the late hour, were trailing bands of squalling children as they haggled for the best price on strings of garlic, vine-ripened tomatoes or a small, straggly bunch of carrots. There were few men of working or fighting age, but here and there, knots of elder males sat in groups smoking their rough, hand-rolled cigarettes and staring straight through the passing foot patrols of People's Polizia and their Red Army escorts. Ivanov and Franco hung back in the entrance to a dogleg alley running off the rear of the piazza, obscured from view by a curtain of bed sheets hung out to dry from the lowest landing of an external staircase. It reminded Ivanov of the fire escapes you found clinging to the side of apartment buildings in places like New York, except this one was made of wood. A fire hazard, not a fire escape.

"She will return soon," said Franco, anticipating his next question. "She is a good girl, my cousin Carlo's daughter. She will bring us what we need."

The Russian did not reply. He merely nodded as he watched the crowd in the marketplace through a gap in the bedclothes, while weighing the heft of the new weapon in his right hand. He'd had to improvise: a heavy cobblestone, ripped up from the road surface and dropped into a gray, tattered pillowcase. A few twirls of the cotton sack and he had a workable cosh. A good weapon for killing without bloodshed. Well, without too much bloodshed.

Ivanov had not spent a great deal of time on the streets of Soviet-controlled Rome. He took in as much detail as he could now, trying not to compare what he saw with what he knew of Free Rome. The poor lighting threw a dire, malarial shroud over the scene, rendering the sunken cheeks and hollow eyes of the women into monstrous caricatures. He needed to understand this part of the city on its own merits, not as a comparison with the Allied sector. It was not easy, because the differences were striking. The Italians, as always, were noisy – they haggled and bickered, loudly talking over each other, gesticulating with their hands – but their efforts were less theatrical here than in the south; more earnest, or even desperate. The children were not starving, exactly, but they had the look of hungry animals about them, a pinched intensity that Ivanov was familiar with from his travels through the outer wastes of Stalin's empire. Their mothers and grandmothers, too, looked malnourished, but worse than that, they looked ashamed of their inability to feed and properly clothe their half-feral children.

Despite the palpable air of anger and despair, however, the city's Communist overlords had it locked down. Ivanov, with long experience in fomenting dissent and insurrection amongst people like this, felt none of the dry, explosive tension in the air that preceded an outburst of mass violence. The menacing presence of heavily armed security patrols saw to that. Their reputation for swift and terrible violence guaranteed it. Every night, the authorities put extra men on the street about an hour before the traditional start of *passeggiatto*. A public order measure, according to the mayor's office, but in reality a bullying tactic. Increasingly the patrols had taken to arresting strollers for minor, summary offenses. Offenses which carried harsh punishments behind the Wall – in addition to the random beatings that often accompanied arrest.

He edged back into the darkness as a couple of machine-gun toting *polizia*, escorted by four soldiers – paratroopers, by the look of their bloused pants and jump boots – stomped by the entrance to their alleyway. They showed no interest in the hiding place, as Furedi had assured him they would not. "They will not come down here," he'd said. "The snout of a pig, it can always be drawn to a sweeter-smelling treat."

This would have been so much easier on the other side of the Wall. Free Rome was a shambles. A mad, anarchic tangle of locals and foreigners, refugees, migrants and the soldiers of six NATO divisions all tumbled in on top of each other. Bands of gypsies ran wild there, often battling with Jewish street gangs and Roman *sgherri*, all of them looking not to get stomped into the pavement by the police or neighborhood mafia enforcers like Franco Furedi. A freak show like that was always easy to hide in. Once you emerged above ground in North Rome, on the other hand, you were in a great open-air prison camp with guards and patrols everywhere. It was a bleak still life, painted in ashen gray, compared to the riot of color and noise across the Wall.

"She comes," whispered Franco.

Ivanov could see nothing of the girl amongst the mass of shoppers and stallholders. Having been alerted by his mafioso guide, though, he faded back into the shadows as arranged, hiding himself in the crawlspace between two dwellings that almost met at the bend in the alley. Franco calmly strolled into the centre of the road surface further back in the alleyway and lay face-down on the cobblestones.

He heard the girl a few moments before he saw her. A lilting, singsong voice, but cracked at the edges with a note of distress. She was speaking to someone in Italian, throwing in the occasional word of Russian. Ivanov settled into a comfortable stance, holding the weighted pillowcase in his dominant hand, ready to move.

Bed sheets ruffled as the laundry parted to let through the girl and her mark. The old, rusting S-shaped street lamps silhouetted them briefly in weak, jaundiced light. Ivanov stood as still as the ancient, red-washed walls around him now. The girl's voice grew more frantic and he saw her hand, one finger extended, pointing at the ground where Franco lay.

"*Eccolo*," she said, sounding scared and upset, "*è morto, tovarishch.*"

Like a dream of a small, ragged angel of death, she moved into his field of view, jabbing her finger at the "dead" body and jumping up and down. She made sure to place herself on the other side of her companion, drawing his eyes away from where Ivanov had concealed himself between the two buildings. He wondered how often the girl had done this and what ruses she used to lure men into a trap when her older cousin was not available to play dead. It was hard to tell her age. She looked underfed and may have been anywhere between eight and twelve years old. But she was a good actress. She drew her prey deep into the killing field and finally Ivanov could see him outlined in the gloom.

He was alone. A tall man, dressed in civilian clothes under his trench coat – one of the lapels of which, no doubt, bore a small red badge that marked him as an NKVD man. She took the stranger by the hand, leading him toward Franco's 'corpse'. He took one step forward, then stopped, seeming to realize where he was. But it was too late. Ivanov was already emerging from the black shadows to his left.

Pavel Ivanov had seen this so many times before: the eyes going wide, the mouth forming an 'O'. A sort of electric jolt that shot through the body as it flooded with adrenaline and made ready to flee or fight. All too late. The NKVD man only had time for dying, which he did quietly.

Ivanov swung the heavy cosh in a short arc. A swift, vicious strike. He felt the mantle of bone collapse like an insect crushed underfoot. Blood spots, a few chips of cranial plate and flecks of meat sprayed out toward the child, who merely stepped to one side as the black-clad foreigner dropped toward the ground. His body twitched and heaved as Ivanov grabbed him and whipped the twisted rope of the pillowcase around his neck to strangle what remained of his life out of the man. Little remained.

His bowels let go with a rich stink, and Ivanov cursed, causing the girl to smile. Her teeth showed startlingly white.

"Quick, help me. I need his clothes before they are too soiled," he said.

Having peeled himself up off the cobblestones, Franco hurried over to his young relative, smiling and patting her on the head as if to congratulate the girl on a good report card. He handed over a small wad of American dollars and a couple of boiled sweets. The girl wiped the dead man's blood off her face with one of the sheets hanging across the alleyway. She kissed the back of Franco's hand and skipped off to find her friends or perhaps her family.

"A good girl, like I told you," said the Roman, as he helped drag the body deeper into the alley, tugging off the trousers as he did so. Ivanov heard shouting and a crash from the market square. He tensed, but Franco shook his head, grunting as he heaved at the dead weight.

"A sweet treat for the pigs – a distraction on the other side of the piazza," he explained. "You must hurry, Russian, this will give us a few minutes. Nothing more. They will be looking for this man soon."

The one-time Spetsnaz officer was already stepping out of the clothes the old woman had brought him an hour ago. Franco was right: cousin Carlo's little girl had done well. The dead man was about his size, dressed in a dark-colored suit and shirt, and a black tie and ankle boots. As Ivanov undressed, Furedi stripped the corpse, grimacing at the fecal leakage.

"It is not too bad," said Ivanov. "Everyone stinks here anyway ... The Russians, I mean," he added when the other man frowned at him.

Only somewhat mollified, Franco searched the clothes for loot before handing the outer garments over to Ivanov. He took money, a fighting knife, a pistol and some documents for himself or his bosses.

"I will need those papers," Ivanov told him.

Franco considered this for a moment, before nodding. "*Sì*. You will."

The dead man's clothes were a little tight on Ivanov, but they would do. And at least they weren't overly stained with blood and gore. As he dressed, he could hear the sounds of some mild disturbance in the marketplace, Italian and Russian voices raised in anger.

"You are certain about this, my friend?" Franco asked. "If you do this, I cannot help you. Nobody from my family, not Marius, not my cousin Carlo's little girl, will come with you. And my family is large."

"And helpful," Ivanov said with a smile, as he did up the buttons on his new shirt. Absentmindedly, he flicked a small blob of gray matter off the collar of his trench coat. His equipment satchel, soiled and ragged, did not match the clothes and he pondered how best to wear it, before removing the MP5 and shortening the strap to carry the submachine gun openly. The satchel he wore around his neck and partly concealed under the trench coat. "Skarov has two companies of NKVD troopers in the tunnels looking for you and me now," he said while rearranging his equipment. "I am better up here. And I still have work to do. Thank you, Franco."

He put out his hand to shake and the Italian took it. The other man's fingers were long and thin, but they gripped with the strength of a crushing machine. He inspected Ivanov's new ensemble and nodded approval. It would do.

"I shall rejoin, Marius," he said. "No matter what happens up here, Russian, you should not try to follow us. You will be lost underground."

"I know," he said. "I will get myself back through the Wall. But my mission was the man in that hotel. I need to know whether he is dead, whether he left anything behind worth coming here for."

"If we kill many Communists tonight, it was worth your coming," Franco replied. He rolled the corpse up against the base of an apartment building wall and tossed Ivanov's discarded clothes on top of it. "Be gone now, Russian," he said finally.

"And the body?"

"It will be gone soon too."

* * *

He walked.

He walked quickly through streets devoid of any joy. Building up his mental map of the city on this side of the Wall. Taking refuge every now and then down blind alleys or in the entrances to deserted businesses. The further north he travelled, the less he saw any evidence of urgency and alarm. Skarov was concentrating his search ever closer to the border with the free city, throwing hundreds of men into the hunt both above and below ground.

Still, there was danger hereabouts. Without the protective magic of Franco Furedi's presence to envelop him, Ivanov soon felt the dull glare of Roman hatred. They watched him from behind shuttered windows and twitching curtains. Their eyes burned dark, like cold embers with all the heat squeezed down beneath black layers of carbon. Dressed as he was, he walked the streets not just as a Russian, but as an agent of Lavrenty Beria, a minion of the Great Satan, as the NKVD *boyar* had come to be known in this deeply Catholic and captive nation. An irony that amused the uptimer, in a grim fashion. Another piece of detritus that had drifted into the past and been taken up by the temps without regard for its origin.

With the occupying forces, he had no trouble at all. To don the cloak of the NKVD was to armor himself in layers of fear and loathing. Even the larger combined patrols of People's Polizia and Red Army overseers went out of their way to avoid him. Nobody wanted the lidless eye of the Great Satan turning on them. Once or twice he saw others of "his" kind – dark-suited men, inevitably wrapped in long trench coats, often with wide-brimmed black hats pulled down somewhat theatrically to hide their eyes. Just as mere mortals steered well clear of him, Ivanov was vigilant in avoiding encounters with any actual agents of the Soviet secret police. Nor did they seek him out. The purpose of their spectral presence on the streets of the enslaved capital was to intimidate. These figures, all cloaked in black, suddenly appearing on the street in front of one's home or place of work, helped to maintain a constant, low-grade current of fear among the population of North Rome. "Stalkers" Franco had called them. One more small, broken piece of meaning from the future.

Only once did Ivanov slip up, later in the evening, when the streets were entirely deserted save for the presence of security patrols. He was walking east along Via Rodi, intending to turn north and head back toward Sobeskaia's hotel when he judged it prudent. A man emerged unexpectedly, almost on top of him, from behind a marble column.

"A word, comrade," he said, startling Ivanov.

Before he could suppress his reaction, he had turned to face the interloper, a man dressed much like him, stiffening his fingers into a spear hand and ...

Then he opened a small gate in his mind, somewhere deep down inside the ancient reptilian brain centers, and allowed his tension to sluice out.

"I startled you," said the NKVD man. "My apologies."

"It is the Romans," Ivanov replied. "I feel them watching me all the time. You know how it is."

His "colleague" stepped down onto the footpath and nodded. "I do," he said. "But I believe the idea is for us to watch them all the time."

Ivanov felt ridiculously naked without a hat to obscure his face like this cheap, comic thug. He turned away from his gaze, pretending to search the street as he spoke. No sense letting the man get a good a look at him. His picture was all over the USSR; it was probably just the darkness and a lack of context that was protecting him from being outed as one of Beria's most wanted targets right now.

He hefted and resettled the MP5, hiding it in plain sight. The equipment satchel under his overcoat felt ungainly and obvious, but the other Stalker appeared to pay it no attention.

"Kuznetzov says they would not dare harm one of us," the OSS operative said, invoking the name of the NKVD station chief in Rome. "But they seem to take *polizia* and stupid farm-boy soldiers with impunity." He pointed off in the direction of the Vatican. "I heard of another corpse in the Tiber tonight. From a patrol I passed earlier."

The other man bristled. "Such talk is not helpful, comrade," he warned. "You should know that. It is defeatist."

"It is," sighed Ivanov, getting into character, but looking all the time for a way to escape this encounter.

A few moments passed with neither man speaking.

"I do not believe we have met before, comrade," the other said at last. "It is odd. I know all the Commisariat men in this district. Are you from Borchov's detail?"

"Of course you do not know me," said Ivanov. "This is not my district. I am carrying a safe-hand message from Colonel-General Skarov for the station chief himself."

"On foot, through this part of the city?" The man seemed incredulous at the thought. "Why not despatch a rider? Is it not urgent?"

"There are no riders, comrade. Do you not know of what is happening by the Wall – or are you so out of touch in District 3? The colonel-general fights a great battle under the city, with the American's hired gangsters from La Cosa Nostra. All our resources are being poured into that fight."

The man stared at him. Saying nothing.

Ivanov felt the meaning of the world shift, just a little, as recognition finally bloomed in the secret policeman's eyes.

"You! Ivano—"

The Spetsnaz officer drove an open-handed strike into his throat in one blurred motion. His victim choked out a dying gasp as Pavel Ivanov's hand closed around his chin and the back of his head, snapping it free of the spinal column with one quick and savage twisting movement. The NKVD goon was dead before Ivanov realised he'd killed him.

He swore quietly, unaware of just how tense he had been up until that moment.

A quick check up and down the street, as he lowered the body onto the footpath, revealed no witnesses. Or none that cared. During his time with Franco, he'd come to appreciate that many eyes could follow one's progress through the occupied city.

Now he looked about for somewhere to dispose of the body.

10

South Rome (Allied sector)

"Inappropriate and off topic, I know," said Harry, as the agent led him away from the angry Russians at reception, "but would you be ...?"

"Plunkett," replied the David Gower lookalike. "David Plunkett."

"David ...?"

"Gower was, would have been, my nephew. By way of my sister. But he's not been born yet, of course. Perhaps never will be. Does the head in, doesn't it, Your Highness?"

"Please. Just Harry. I'm not nearly so high and mighty as I once was. The line of succession took a long detour around me in '48." Having touched on the mind-fucking confusion of his father not being conceived in this world, and where that left him in the royal food chain, Harry steered the conversation back to the Plunkett family tree. "Don't you find it a bit difficult in this line of work, having a famous unborn nephew? A doppelganger, really. You could be his twin."

They had pushed far enough into Babington's to have left behind the protests and shouts of Beria's men, but were not yet into the crush and roar of the party proper. A few guests turned and, recognizing Harry, raised their drinks and smiled. Some of the men dipped their heads and a few of the women even curtsied, which wasn't at all necessary – in fact, it was a breach of protocol, strictly speaking. The Act of Succession that removed him, or rather clarified his irrelevance to the royal line in this world, had made all such ceremony redundant. Harry didn't mind his redundancy one little bit.

"I'm a declared asset," said Plunkett. "MI6 liaison to the host government. Wouldn't have worked out that way originally, from what I've been told. But we play the cards as they are dealt."

"Or each ball on its own merits."

"Indeed," the not-so-secret agent agreed with a smile. "Her Majesty's government had already invested considerable time and money in my early training when the penny dropped. Would have been a terrible waste to just let me go when I could play at being the most dangerous concierge in Europe."

"Well then, I suppose we'd best not fuck around," said Harry. He could feel the hardened carapace of his old operational psyche clamping itself around him. Outwardly he remained a smiling, pleasant supernumerary, breezing in to a party to glad-hand and bullshit the guests in about equal measure. Inside, he was already preparing himself to deal damage and absorb whatever punishment came back at him.

The atmosphere in the restaurant was strange. The wait staff, said Plunkett, were operating under orders to bring out as much alcohol as quickly as they could, especially to any Russians in need of a drink. Nobody offered the SIS man or Harry as much as a shandy, and he doubted they'd give him a drink even if he had asked. The Russians too, he noted, in defiance of national character, were remaining resolutely dry.

"So, how many of these cheeky fuckers do we have in here?" Harry asked.

"The Smedlovs? Nine that we're aware of. That's nine hitters. The better part of an NKVD snatch squad that got in before we could stop them, and a couple of ring-ins from their embassy's undeclared asset list. Plus another five guests here legitimately, from the trade delegation to the conference."

Plunkett led him through the heaving press of the crowd. Harry followed close at heel. "And our assets?" he asked.

"I have two close protection details in here," said Plunkett. "Ten men each. And we have some freelance help," he added, with the trace of a grin.

"OSS?"

"Hardly," said Plunkett. "A chap from your old shop, actually."

"The Regiment? Smashing. Can we expect any trouble from the trade ministry people?" Harry asked.

He was aware of being tracked by two Slavic-looking bruisers, who were keeping pace with him and Plunkett as they moved further into the venue. The goons were not shy about muscling their way through the crowd. He could track their progress by the drinks they spilled, the elbows jostled, and by one old dame they nearly knocked to the ground. Under different circumstances, Harry might have hurried over to help her up, and popped the Bolshevik enforcer a good one on the nose for his bad manners. Instead he hurried along just behind the SIS agent. The Russians were radiating a nasty vibe throughout the gathering. Harry was alive to it, and increasingly so were the guests.

"Hard to say what they might do if and when things kick off," Plunkett conceded of the five Soviet diplomats. "We have pretty thorough coverage on all of them. As best we can tell, there are no real players there. A couple with military experience, because – well, who doesn't nowadays? But nothing of note. And we have each of them marked, anyway. It's Beria's people who are making a bloody nuisance of themselves."

By now Harry could see for himself what Plunkett meant. He recognized the British ambassador – backed into a corner, engaged in an animated discussion with a short, balding character, who seemed to be leaking sweat from every pore in his body. The man's cheap, ill-fitting suit shone where the light caught it, and his frightened eyes darted back and forth between another pair of slab-shouldered Soviet brutes, who were doing their best to slowly, surreptitiously, force their way through a cordon of Plunkett's people. The human bag of sweat and nerves was none other than Valentin Sobeskaia.

From this distance, the contest between the Russians and the embassy's security people was fascinating to behold. It had not come to open blows yet, but Beria's men were not far off. The larger of the two was toe to toe with an enormous black man, whose dinner jacket probably cost more than the Russian earned in a year.

Harry smiled. In fact he almost laughed out loud at the sight of his former regimental sergeant-major, and his spirits lifted for the first time since he had seen Julia, so many hours before.

"Viv," he said, rolling the name around in his mouth like a boiled sweet. "Plunkett, we are in rare good luck. Everything is going to be fine. Or not. But better than I'd thought, anyway."

"Indeed. Mr. St Clair is here in a private capacity, as a businessman, of course ..."

Harry waved off Plunkett's explanation. "Oh, I'm not at all surprised that Viv would be mixed up in all this."

"I'll gather more troops, if you think you're good for this, sir?" said the SIS man.

"Good to go," Harry replied, as he watched the big West Indian shift his center of gravity slightly, while holding on to the wrist of the NKVD thug attempting to get past him. The former SAS noncom drew the other man's hand across his body and inflated his chest with a deep breath. The move was quick and almost impossible to see, if you didn't know what to look for. But Harry could hear the crack as St Clair broke the man's elbow. The Russian's face turned yellow, then white. Sweat beaded his high forehead and the muscles in his jaw line knotted as he ground his teeth together.

But he did not retreat. Instead, he used his close proximity to St Clair to attempt a killing blow. Harry saw the flash of a blade appear in his good hand just in time. It looked like an oyster knife, stolen from the buffet.

"Viv, old man! On your left," he called out, distracting both Russians but not St Clair. It was not his first bar fight, after all. St Clair ratcheted up the torque on the arm lock as Harry lunged forward and grabbed the attacker's knife hand, crushing it back into the joint and twisting viciously, breaking that limb too. The NKVD hard man groaned and staggered away from the confrontation. He looked as if he was about to vomit.

"Bloody Russians," said Harry. "Never could handle their drink. Or the cutlery."

"Nice to see you, guv," beamed his old sergeant. "Heads up ..."

The West Indian interposed himself between Harry and the second attacker, who had moved up quietly on his blind side. St Clair's hand shot out and back-fisted the man in the testicles. Harry flinched when he heard the crack. Plunkett took the victim by the arm, not gently, and propeled him away from the ambassador and Comrade Sobeskaia.

"Nasty," Harry muttered, with a heartfelt grimace. "I think I heard one of his goolies pop."

"That's disappointing, guv," said St Clair. "I was shooting for both."

Harry looked down as he felt a hand gripping his bicep. It was Sobeskaia, who had detached himself from the ambassador.

"Your Highness, you must get me out of here. You must get me away. They mean to kill me. I know what they're capable of. We must go." The guy was dangerously close to babbling.

"Oh, I think we all know what they're capable of. Get a grip, man – but not on me." Harry prised the Russian businessman's fingers from his upper arm. Sobeskaia's hands were cold and clammy. Panic sweat.

"Don't mind him, guv," said St Clair. "I've got him covered."

The ambassador, an ex-Royal Navy man, Harry recalled, did his best to calm their would-be defector and to draw him away from Harry and Viv, who had now been targeted by three more NKVD goons.

"Come, Mr. Sobeskaia. It's a little crowded here by the buffet. Come stand with me, would you?"

Harry took up station next to the forbidding presence of Vivian Richards St Clair – 6 foot 4 inches of hard-packed West Indian carnivore. The reception roared on around them, largely oblivious to the quietly violent struggle playing out near the sausage rolls and party pies. Harry understood now why Carstairs and Walker had not let him bring a weapon other than the pig sticker strapped along his forearm. It would be too tempting to open up on the Smedlovs, and God knows how many bystanders would've been cut down in the crossfire. He supposed the only reason the Sovs hadn't opened up on Sobeskaia was thanks to the metal detector out in the foyer. They hadn't been able to get any artillery inside, contemporary ceramics and plastic munitions being what they were. Which is to say, complete arse.

They must have wanted this character back quite badly, though. Because while everybody was keeping things relatively nice on the surface, beneath that it was obvious they intended to either escort Sobeskaia out of the reception or leave his corpse behind.

"What are you even doing here, Viv?" Harry asked as they watched the approach of the three Soviet strongmen.

"Just trying to turn a quid, governor," said his one-time NCO. "I've got a lot of old boys from the barracks on my books now, you know. Turned over a mill in profit last year for the first time – after tax, of course. Not easy to do with Her Majesty's Inland Revenue having its paws so deep in my funds. Oh, no offense, guv."

"None taken, Sergeant. Wakey wakey, here comes trouble ..."

The NKVD emerged from the jostle of the crowd in a two-up, one-back formation, hoping to engage Harry and St Clair in defending themselves and Sobeskaia from the first attackers, while the third slipped in with a blade or perhaps a poison point, whatever they intended to use on him. Harry caught himself nervously running his thumb over his fingertips, anticipating the confrontation before it arrived. He breathed in and out and tried to empty his mind. To play the ball on its own merits, as he had said to Plunkett. He waited, knees slightly bent, his weight focused forward on the balls of his feet, eyes settled on the center mass of the man who seemed to be coming directly at him.

Before the Russians could reach him, Harry stepped out and closed the distance between them, shifting off-line just before their bodies met, fending away the slashing blade that tried to open him up. He turned outside the short arc described by the knife, stamping down on the Russian's instep with the heel of his expensive Italian loafers. Bones cracked and the man grunted, but not without trying to drive an elbow into Harry's solar plexus. He foiled that with a high-low block that appeared to most onlookers as though he was patting a friend on the shoulder, and perhaps directing him toward the food table with a gentle push on the elbow. In fact, he had unsheathed his own blade and buried it deep into the tricep of the other man, who lost control of his weapon hand and dropped his blade to the floor.

St Clair, he noticed in his peripheral vision, appeared to have a friendly arm around the shoulder of his Smedlov, and was swinging him around, laughing as though he had just been told a particularly ribald joke. The third man, who was making directly for Sobeskaia, suddenly found his approach blocked by the dead weight of his colleague, whose neck had been snapped by the former SAS sergeant. The dead man – he was most certainly dead, thought Harry – dropped to the floor, tripping the last NKVD agent and a waiter carrying a tray of drinks. The enormous crash of shattering glass brought a momentary lull to the roaring buzz of the party, but only for a second or two. Plunkett appeared with a couple of offsiders, raised both eyebrows at the carnage in the corner, and tut-tutted Harry.

"The idea was rather to *avoid* an incident, you know."

"He choked on a particularly long ribbon sandwich," Harry replied, nodding at the body of the Russian spy on the floor.

Plunkett's people were already muscling away the walking wounded from Beria's snatch team. Or hit squad. Or whatever they were. Most of the onlookers who had no idea what was going on backed off. A couple of them offered their medical expertise, and one woman fanned herself into a complete faint. Adding to the confusion.

"This is all a bit of a fucking dog's breakfast really," Harry declared. "Viv, watch my back would you?"

He turned on Sobeskaia, taking him by the lapel and dragging him away from the ambassador.

"You couldn't even be bothered wearing a proper dinner jacket," he rebuked the terrified *boyar*. "Typical. I hope you're going to be bloody worth it, my friend. With me – we're out of here. Now."

Harry propeled the Russian toward a pair of swinging doors from which waiters would occasionally emerge with trays of drinks and canapé. He shot an inquiry back over his shoulder at Plunkett. "You secured the kitchens, right?"

"Of course."

"Marvelous. Let's go."

The sudden movement, on top of the excitement of the recent confrontation, sent waves of confusion and concern through the packed masses inside Babington's. A stone's throw from the showdown with the NKVD, it would have been impossible to know what was happening; but people on the other side of the room soon knew that *something* was happening. A sudden sparkle of flash photography lit the room. For just a moment Harry experienced the dizzying shift of perspective that all the uptimers knew so well. He flinched away from the brief, strobing white light, convinced he was being photographed on dozens of smart phones and uploaded to the net in real time.

He wasn't, but the conviction was hard to shake.

Harry dragged Sobeskaia along behind him, with the huge bulk of Vivian Richards St Clair providing protection in the rear while Plunkett kept a watching brief. The confused babble of the party guests quickly increased as the remaining Russians attempted to follow. SIS muscle intervened, leading to some ugly pushing and shoving, which generated further shouts of complaint and cries from distressed bystanders. Harry let it all fall behind him as he pulled the defector into the kitchens, almost knocking another waiter to the floor, and grabbing a handful of devils on horse-back as he hurried past an unattended platter of food. He was starving and grateful for the sugary protein hit.

A waitress screamed and he realized his white dress shirt was covered in the blood of the man he'd stabbed in the arm. So much for discretion.

"Thank you, thank you," Sobeskaia kept babbling. "Thank you, Prince Harry."

"He's not really a prince anymore, you know," said St Clair, in disturbingly good humor. "He's more of a celebrity really. Like you'd find on *The Apprentice*, if you had any decent fucking telly here."

"Try not to do his head in, please, Viv. There might be something in there we need later."

"What is this? What does this mean?" Sobeskaia asked, panicked.

There was a scuffle at the doors behind them, and Plunkett begged off to join his people in neutralizing the other Soviet gatecrashers.

"Oh, just in case I don't get a chance later on, sir ... er, *Harry*," the David Gower lookalike said. "It's been cracking good fun working with you, despite the chaos and madness and the general air of cocking everything up." But he said it with a boyish grin, which Harry recognized from his own extensive repertoire.

The two ex-commandos now hurried their charge over to a fire exit.

"Thank you, my prince, thank you," he continued to babble.

"Oh, for fuck's sake," said Harry. "Don't make me roll my eyes ..." Then he turned to St Clair. "Have a bit of a stickybeak out there in the alley, would you, Viv? See if there're any villains lying in wait."

"Got it, guv," he said, before slipping out through the fire door.

Only now did Harry give Sobeskaia his full attention for the first time. "Right. Listen up, you. I don't know what fucking game you're playing. I don't know what you've got that you think we might need. But if you want to get out of this place alive, you're going to tell me now. Not a week from now, or during the debrief. Right fucking now."

11

North Rome (Soviet sector)

Ivanov muscled the dead weight of the corpse back into the shadows under the building's portico. The NKVD man's bladder and bowels had let go in death. Ivanov dragged the body by its head, which he had snapped free of the spinal column. The loose, detached feeling of dragging so much mass around on a thin column of ruptured meat was unsettling, but not unfamiliar. He was cautious not to befoul himself with the man's bodily wastes. The clothes he had stolen from his last victim were already a little rank.

Taking a moment to scope out his surroundings, Ivanov considered his options. Via Rodi traversed the Soviet sector, from the south-west to the north-east about six blocks north of the Wall, where it abutted the edge of the Vatican. There were fewer apartments in this part of the city, the buildings tending toward larger, boxy modern structures given over to official use. It was, thankfully, something of a dead zone at this time of night. There were fewer witnesses to raise an alarm and fewer eyes to follow his progress as he attempted to exfiltrate the area. There were also, unfortunately, far fewer options to dispose of the body. This part of North Rome was not like the rats' nest Franco had led him through earlier, with hundreds of dark, twisting alleys and Byzantine passageways in which he might hide a multitude of sins.

Ivanov scanned up and down the quiet street, his eyes playing over the blank, unlit façades. Leafless trees stood sentinel outside the anonymous-looking buildings, most of them five or six stories high. Unlike the streets of Free Rome, which were gridlocked with traffic day and night, very few vehicles were parked along Via Rodi. He counted two vans in the livery of the city government, one slab-sided Trabant sedan and, away in the distance, what looked like a horse-drawn cart. Without horses. Nowhere suggested itself as a quick and dirty dumping ground for a recently murdered secret policeman.

Ivanov was beyond overwatch. He could not call in the cleaners as he might in the Allied sector. He couldn't even stuff the corpse into a garbage bin. For the duration of the GATT conference, the local authorities removed all the trash cans and dumpsters from the streets at the end of each day. The regime declared it a security measure, and rounded up a hundred or so "suspected insurgents" to back up the claim, but really they just wanted to discourage any scavenging by the city's impoverished and hungry inmates. It was not a good look for a worker's paradise.

He examined the doors of the building in front of which he stood. They were massive, nearly twice as tall as him, constructed of dark hardwood and securely padlocked. No joy to be had there.

There was nothing for it. He resolved to simply drag the body a little deeper into the shadows and abandon it. A quick search yielded up some currency, a Makarov pistol with two spare clips, and a transit pass that would allow him free use of any form of public transport. He pocketed the weapons and ammo, and took the man's wallet. The transit pass was of marginal usefulness. The buses and trains in the Soviet sector ran sporadically, but fares were cheap. He could afford to ride them for a month with the cash he had in his pockets.

He found the dead man's NKVD credentials in a leather flip-out style holder inside the breast pocket of the overcoat. His name was Stanislav Borodin, a *sergant special'noy* with the People's Commissariat for Internal Affairs. Roughly translated: a master sergeant in the NKVD's "special services" division. Ivanov pocketed that next to the ID he had taken from the body of Borodin's colleague back at the market square. Neither of the deceased looked like him in life, death or the black-and-white photo IDs, but very few people were apt to examine the documents too closely, and as a free pass within Occupied Rome, they beat the hell out of a bus ticket.

He dragged Borodin as far back into the shadows as he could and arranged the body to look like he was sleeping off a drinking binge. It was not unknown among the occupying forces, although it was rare for Beria's men to behave so unprofessionally. Such foolishness was almost inevitably fatal. If the Great Satan himself did not see to your demise, the local population almost certainly would.

Ivanov set off once more, drifting east and then south toward Via Giordano Bruno. Back in July 1943, partisans in this part of the city had staged a brief but intense last stand against the Red Army paratroopers who had jumped into Rome when the fascist regime fell apart. Strange bedfellows these resistance fighters had been. Gangs of criminals, demobilized soldiers who had held on to their weapons, anarchists, and even some local Communists who had sided with Trotsky decades before. There had also been rumors of Allied special operators fighting alongside the Italians, in order to delay and frustrate a complete Soviet takeover of Rome. Ivanov had been working with the Office of Strategic Services since the end of the war and he had heard most of these rumors from fellow operatives. None of them, however, ever laid claim to having been on the ground here at the time.

The burned-out shells of buildings, large piles of rubble and occasional overgrown, weed-choked lots on both sides of Giordano Bruno spoke of high-intensity urban warfare. The Russians had done well to confine it to a few blocks, although the partisans had aided in preserving the wider city by not spreading and escalating their fight. To the trained eye of a Spetsnaz officer, the rumors of OSS and British Special Operations Executive involvement looked less like wishful thinking as he strode through the ruined district. Stalin's forces had bled out here for two weeks, and yet a couple of blocks away, the eternal city appeared untouched by war, the Transition and even time itself. Maybe there was some truth to the stories.

Moving slowly in the direction of the Wall, Ivanov reviewed the situation. He had elected to make his own crossing back to Free Rome, without the support of Franco's people or whatever network the elder Furedi was running. The Roman Wall was not impenetrable; it was merely very difficult to cross above ground, under the muzzles of the machine guns in the watchtowers. That was the escape route normal people took, and that was how so many contemporary Romans had died. But the Furedis had shown him there were alternatives. He just didn't know how to navigate them.

He slowed down as a six-wheeled troop carrier rumbled through an intersection two blocks ahead. The vehicle commander was buttoned up inside, Ivanov noticed, in defiance of the Red Army mandate that officers ride uncovered while on patrol, head out of the hatch. But he was obviously a wiser man than the superiors who issued a standing order that amounted to an invitation to be sniped. The big diesel engines of the BMP grunted and roared as it coughed oily smoke from its exhausts and rolled on into the night.

With the money, transit pass and ID lifted from the men he had killed, Ivanov did have the option of laying low in the occupied sector, or even of going deeper into Communist northern Italy. That he was expressly barred from doing so by his OSS handlers was of minor concern. They were using him, and he was using them. In the end, only results would matter. Sobeskaia had given the OSS enough of a fright to put Ivanov into North Rome, the first time in many years the Americans had let him operate within the Eastern Bloc. Whatever the businessman had to offer, they wanted it. And Ivanov wanted it too.

His track had taken him through the bomb-blasted, skeletal remains of three blocks along Via Giordano Bruno. Quite abruptly, he now entered a neighborhood less ravaged by the previous decade's street fighting. Here the apartment buildings were covered in scaffolding; a cement truck and a small crane, both of them locked up for the night, were further signs of local reclamation work. Within another block, he'd left behind all evidence of the small, intimate war that had once been fought here. Between Vias Ostia and Candia, the only damage had been done by the dead hand of Soviet occupation. The heavy, drab graying out of any color or sense of vibrancy in the streetscape was consistent with the rest of Communist-controlled Rome. But at least the fabric of the city had not been torn apart. Once the Stalinists were driven out, life would return. Real life.

A helicopter thudded through the night a mile or so away. A big Hind gunship, by the sound of it, apparently patrolling in a long lazy arc. A searchlight stabbed down at one point, but blinked out again almost immediately – a routine procedure, to remind citizens that they were forever under surveillance. If the chopper crew had been searching for a particular target, they would've lanced it with the spotlights and possibly opened up with miniguns. There had been no such incidents since the start of the trade conference, but Ivanov did not doubt that should one of the gunships catch Franco and his colleagues out in the open, image management would quickly give way to an opportunistic firestorm.

He checked his watch. It was late, many hours since he had broken contact with that dog Skarov. The relative quiet on the streets and the apparent concentration of occupying forces near the Wall gave him to believe that Skarov had poured his resources into pursuing the Romans there, hoping to bottle them up before they could escape via their maze of underground passages. Even as he argued with himself in favor of this conclusion, another helicopter hammered by in the night sky, overhead this time, making for the airspace above the Wall a few blocks to the south. Once there, the Hind took up a holding pattern, occasionally slicing up the streets below with all four of its spotlights.

Forcing himself to maintain a steady, even pace when all of his instincts told him to shy away in the shadows, Ivanov continued on a course toward Sobeskaia's hotel. He had been on the move for nearly twenty-four hours and he was bone tired. No longer a young man, Pavel Ivanov drew on deep reserves of ill will to keep going. The strap of his satchel, still half hidden beneath the overcoat, kept riding up on his neck and digging into his carotid, adding a deep bass note to the thumping headache he already had. Cramps rippled up his legs and into his lower back. But he had to keep moving. The mission was everything. Well, almost everything. There was also the prospect of settling up with Skarov. He *had* to go back to the Albergo Grimaldi.

He turned up the collar of the long black coat and reassured himself there were any number of reasons and justifications he could cite for taking such a risk. Primary amongst them, his failure. He had failed to make contact with the businessman or the man's mistress. He had failed to collect whatever intelligence they had to offer. He had failed to even establish the nature of that offering. The presence of Skarov, the wild, intemperate response of the Communists while the whole world looked toward Rome – these things indicated a measure of desperation on Beria's part. Whatever game was in play here, the stakes were high. It was worth Ivanov taking a risk just to keep playing.

But as he moved back into the streets he had escaped earlier with the help of Franco and Marius and, let's not forget, cousin Carlo's murderous little girl, he knew that all of the reasons and justifications in the world meant nothing really. Only one thing was drawing him back to that hotel, only one man, and it was not Valentin Sobeskaia. It was Colonel-General Skarov of the NKVD. Pavel Ivanov meant to kill him. Maybe he would be at the *albergo*. Maybe not.

His boot heels clicked on ancient flagstones as he advanced, in character as Sergant Special'noy Stanislav Borodin of the NKVD. Perhaps the troopers he'd encounter ahead would recognize him from alerts and bulletins, not to mention the wanted posters that hung in their thousands throughout the USSR and its satellite territories. Perhaps they would sling the submachine guns they carried and open up on him in panic.

Or perhaps he might walk right past them and into the hotel.

12

North Rome (Soviet sector)

There were no primaries at the Albergo Grimaldi. Nobody like Borodin, or Skarov, or himself. Only sleepy guards, and anxious-looking hotel staff. The two conscripts on the front door hurried to shuffle out of his way as he stomped up the steps and reached for his stolen ID. The trench coat, the badge, the air of entitlement and threat were enough for them.

Of course, thought Ivanov, as he adjusted his satchel, dragging it around a little so that it sat on the back of his hip.

The foyer was a mess. Four more troopers lounged around inside, two of them asleep. The other pair played cards and smoked. They started a little when he stalked in but returned to their game when the NKVD man evinced no interest in them. The *albergo*'s entry and reception area was not large and what space there was had been taken up by piles of luggage, suitcases and so on, and by the squaddies' equipment, which included a small gas stove on which they were heating coffee. Probably spiked with vodka, and almost certainly stolen from the hotel stores.

Muddy footprints ran everywhere over the thin red carpet. A couple of lightbulbs had failed, adding to the gloomy atmosphere. A man and a woman, both with the underfed, anxious look of locals about them, worked behind the counter, mostly trying not to catch his eye. Ivanov had Borodin's identity card and badge out by then and bruited his way over to them, jutting his chin out and allowing the contempt that all secret policeman felt for their fellow beings to run free across his features. A brief wave of the NKVD badge was enough to ensure their attention and drain what little color was left in the face of the night manager.

"I am here under the direct orders of district co-ordinator Kuznetzov," he informed them while keeping an eye on the Red Army squad members in the dirty, fly-specked mirror behind the counter. The name of Kuznetzov caught the attention of the corporal who was playing cards and the young man kept one eye on Ivanov while attending to the little gas stove. Like a good Russian, however, he took no initiative to act beyond the orders he had been given. Watch the foyer.

"There was an incident here earlier today," continued Ivanov, in character. "I have flown down from Zagreb to investigate the handling of this matter. I will need to inspect the rooms and property of all involved, and to speak with the controlling officer, Colonel-General Skarov. Where is he?"

The name of Lavrenty Beria's hatchet man caused both troopers to turn his way now, warily, and the poor Romans behind the desk to shake uncontrollably. The man and woman exchanged a nervous glance, and seemed even more nervous for having done so.

"Conrad ... Comrade Skarov is not here," said the man.

The woman clutched at her throat – probably reaching for the rosary beads she dared not wear in public, Ivanov thought.

"He is at the Wall," the night manager added. "There have been incidents. Terrorists and criminals." The woman nodded gravely, still clutching at the religious totem that was not there.

"The keys then," he demanded.

The manager looked confused, perhaps even a bit reluctant. Ivanov glowered at him. "These terrorists, these criminals – you have some sympathy with them, comrade?"

The poor Italian almost choked on his response. "Oh no, no, no ..." he said quickly, while reaching around to pluck two keys from a board on the wall behind him.

Ivanov snatched them out of his hand and stalked away from the counter, stopping to bestow a withering gaze on the corporal, who was staring at him.

"You there, soldier!" he barked.

The man jumped, spilling some of his coffee. Ivanov was certain he could smell ouzo.

"Do you know where Colonel-General Skarov might be? I am to report to him and seek information about what took place here earlier."

The noncom stumbled to his feet. His two sleeping comrades disturbed themselves. "No ..." the corporal said uncertainly, before adding with more vigor: "No, comrade. We were detailed here when your section was finished with the scene. Partisans attacked today. They are everywhere in this part of the city. We are to secure the hotel against them."

Ivanov stared at the steaming coffee he held. "Good job," he said dryly. "What can you tell me of the partisan attack? Quickly now, I must be about my investigations."

"It was a serious attack," the other man replied. "They came up through the sewers. We heard that many of Colonel-General Skarov's men were killed down there. The colonel chases them now. That is what we hear, anyway. But the NKVD does not always inform us of details. We have been given orders, comrade. To stay here in the foyer. That is really all I know. If you cannot find Colonel-General Skarov, it is because he is in pursuit of the partisans."

Ivanov allowed himself to look slightly dissatisfied with the answer. It rang true. Skarov was not a man to step back from the blow that the Furedi brothers had delivered to him this afternoon. He would take it as a personal affront and a failure. Ivanov was familiar with that way of thinking.

With a wave, he dismissed the soldier, who cautiously resumed his seat, his card game and his drink. The would-be NKVD master sergeant turned away without another word. He took the stairs to the second floor, where Sobeskaia and his mistress had taken adjoining rooms. The crowded foyer with its piles of luggage and unwashed floor had given the impression of a poorly run, typically drab state hotel. But the muddy footprints petered out on the first landing of the stairwell, and from what he could see of the hallway, the staff had done a better job of maintaining some order up here.

Ten rooms ran off either side of the long corridor, which was well lit and tidy. Halfway down, a small table held a bowl of fruit. That in itself was testimony to a standard of luxury not easily found on this side of the Wall. The apples, pears and grapes looked fresh. It was significant, he thought, that they remained untouched. To provide them in the first place was an uncommon measure of largesse in the Soviet sector; that nobody had stolen every piece of fruit gave some indication that the guests here were more familiar with material ease than the Romans on the streets outside. It also meant, he would bet, that the conscripts he had seen downstairs had not wandered up here. The accommodation fitted with Ivanov's image of Sobeskaia as a privileged *boyar*. At least, until very recently.

He stopped outside room 203, where Anya, the mistress, had stayed. He could hear two guests talking in another room nearby, and the clink of cutlery on dinner plates as somebody ate a room service meal. But nothing from 203. Drawing the pistol he had taken from Borodin, Ivanov enter the room.

It had been professionally searched. The bed was stripped, the mattress flipped. Dresser drawers had been removed and stacked. A watercolor painting leaned against the wall, an outline of its frame showing where it had hung until a few hours ago. He could see no personal effects. There would be nothing here, and probably nothing next door in Sobeskaia's room.

A connecting door gave him access to 204, where he found the scene repeated. The room had been taken apart efficiently, methodically: no personal effects strewn everywhere; no curtains ripped down from the rails; no feathers or foam spilling out from where rough, impatient hands had slashed open the mattress, searching for contraband. There was nothing here for him. Still, it had to be searched, and he did so as thoroughly as whoever had gone through it before.

Ivanov was in the en suite bathroom, lifting the lid on the toilet cistern, when he heard them coming for him. The thunder of boots up the stairs and along the corridor.

He didn't hesitate. Didn't stop to think. He took a grenade from his weapons satchel, pulled the pin, and tossed it through into the bedroom a fraction of a second before he used the heavy ceramic cistern lid to smash open the fixed window of the bathroom. It sounded like all six of the squad members had come for him, but others were with them too.

Skarov. He recognized the devil's voice, muted, out in the hallway.

"Ivanov! Give up. We have you."

But they didn't. He ripped the plastic shower curtain from its moorings, looped it around the thick pipe under the washbasin directly below the broken window. He launched himself through, holding tightly on to the improvised rope, slamming into the side of the hotel a few feet below the sill.

Hobnail boots crashed on a wooden door somewhere above him. He heard it burst inwards and smash against the wall like the crack of a rifle shot a second before the grenade exploded. The entire building shook as he dropped through clear air trailed by the screams of dying men. He seemed to fall forever yet hit the ground immediately, allowing his legs to fold up underneath him, breathing out and dropping into a judo roll as glass and burning splinters rained down around him. The impact slammed up through his ankles and knees like an electric shock. He rolled to his feet and ran, not sure exactly where he was or in which direction he was heading.

He ran – surprised that he could, that a shinbone was not protruding from his lower leg like a broken spear. A single shot rang out and sparked off the cobblestone beside him, but he threw himself to the left and around the corner, out of the line of fire.

Skarov would be coming for him. The NKVD colonel-general would not have led the way into the hotel room, knowing of the danger within. Ivanov cursed himself – his foolishness, his obsession – then he put it all aside and ran, emptying the pockets of the heavy trench coat before stripping it off as he dived into a barely lit, narrow passageway.

More shots, but muted by distance and the buildings that now stood between him and his pursuers. They were firing at shadows, at nothing. He had maybe a minute or two's advantage, a head start before Skarov threw hundreds of men onto the streets of North Rome to find him.

Another left turn and then a right, however, and Ivanov suddenly found his precious advantage was gone.

He had run blindly into a dead end. Darkened tenements rose three and four stories above him; behind him, he could hear shouts and the barking of dogs. At the very edge of perception he was aware of being observed. Not by the men who were now hunting him, but by the city itself. By hundreds of eyes in these darkened tenements. By blank walls, empty windows and shadows.

He checked his satchel. Two Makarovs, the MP5 and night-vision goggles; in his pockets, three clips of ammunition for the pistols. His pursuers were drawing close. Ivanov could hear the engines of motorbikes and a truck, and the deep industrial growl of a troop carrier. He could not risk doubling back out of this cul-de-sac. But he seemed to have no options here, no external fire escapes or trellises he might scale, no open doors through which he could dive.

He was just fitting the NVGs, planning to scan for an entrance to the drains, when he heard her voice.

"Come with me, Russian. Quickly."

He jumped. She had emerged from the pitch-black shadows.

"Who are ...?" And then he recognized her. "Carlo's little girl." It was as much a question as a statement.

"You must come now," she said, urging him into a building entrance he had not noticed before. The heavy steel door stood slightly ajar.

Ivanov moved toward her, but cautiously. "The last Russian who followed you is dead," he said.

"Yes," she replied. As if that ended it. "Come."

He could hear the deep bass thud of inbound choppers. The gunships that had been loitering over the Wall, he was certain. That closed off any debate he may have had with himself.

Ivanov dived into the darkness, following the girl into the building and dragging the heavy door closed behind him. He didn't have a chance to power up the goggles before she'd struck a match and lit a single candle, which looked as though it had come from a church. The lower half of a bright red crucifix design stood out on the half-burnt remnants. The girl shielded the flame with her hand as she led him up a flight of stairs.

"What is your name, girl?" he asked. "I know you only as Franco's cousin."

"You can call me Eva," she said. "Franco is cousin to my papa, but he is very old so I call him uncle. Come now, Russian."

He could hear more vehicles outside, and the shouts of Red Army noncoms and barking dogs. But the dogs were too numerous to all be trackers, surely. It seemed every flea-bitten cur for a mile around had spilled onto the streets.

"Do not worry about the dogs," Eva told him. "They cannot track you."

"What?" Ivanov was momentarily confused, but continued to climb the stairs behind her all the same.

The building seemed to be empty, but he knew that was not true. It was big enough, and generally, he had found, the Romans were crowded into their apartments in such great numbers that up to 300 people may well have been resident here. But he could see no one, other than Eva. She rounded the banister on the very top landing and hurried toward a knotted rope hanging from an attic opening.

"The Stalinists sometimes use dogs to track us," she explained as she blew out the candle and flew up the rope with no more difficulty than she'd had ascending the stairs. "But we have trained our own dogs. They will fall on the handlers and their beasts before they even pick up your scent."

Eva did not relight the candle and Ivanov wasted no time in hauling himself up after her. He was about to fit the goggles again when she reached out and touched his arm, stopping him. It was a curiously adult gesture.

"You will not need them," she said. "And it is better that you do not have them on if the helicopters come with searchlights."

Ivanov did not need that explained to him, but he did need to know where she had come from, and why. "I am in debt to you for your assistance, young lady," he began. "But how is it you came to offer this assistance? It has been many hours since I separated from Franco, and I did not tell him I was returning to the hotel."

Eva was crouched in the attic space, her small face illuminated by a shaft of moonlight pouring in through a hole in the roof. Where she had seemed strangely grown up just a few seconds ago, she now rolled her eyes like a young girl beset by the stupidity of the adult world.

"You are our responsibility, Russian. We have been watching you since you set foot here. We lost you once or twice, but as soon as you returned this way, we picked you up again. Uncle Franco and Father Marius warned me you might come back to the *albergo*, and that it would be my job to guide you away from whatever foolishness and trouble you caused. So come now, Russian, we must go."

For just a moment he was struck dumb and immobile. Ivanov had the unpleasant sensation of perceiving a much greater truth, of snatching a glimpse for a mere second of how he fitted into the machinations of others as a flimsy, disposable cog. And then he heard dogs barking and fighting and the crackle of gunfire nearby, and he put it all aside to follow the girl, who was already on the move.

The wide attic space was cramped overhead, forcing him to move along beneath the centerline of the pitched roof while crouched over. His eyes had readjusted to the darkness, which was split here and there by shafts of silvery light piercing through gaps and holes in the terracotta tiles above them. Much of the space here was taken up with boxes and sacks of supplies. He could smell garlic, as always, but even more strongly, the ubiquitous dried fruit, preserved meat and cheeses. Two rifles, German Mausers from the previous decade's war, were propped up in one corner, visible in a shaft of moonlight.

Wood creaked on wood as Eva pushed against a solid wooden shutter in the roof. Ivanov came up behind her and lent his strength to the task. The skylight squealed open, making him cringe, but the streets were already alive with confusion and noise. He could hear hundreds of men below them, and dozens of vehicles. The dogfighting was over, seemingly coming to an end with the crack of a single pistol shot. He followed Eva out onto the roof line, feeling terribly exposed as he emerged into the bright starlit night.

To the south, the lights of Free Rome twinkled and shimmered like a vast illuminated sea lapping all the way out to the horizon. The dome of St Peter's, lit from below by spotlights, stood out in glorious relief. Even the guard towers of the Roman Wall twinkled as if wrapped in fairy lights.

"Follow me," said the young girl. "Do not stray. A giant oaf like you will fall straight through."

He did as he was told, carefully stepping not just in line with her, but as far as possible in her footsteps. The ancient tiles shifted and once or twice even cracked beneath his weight, but he could feel the solid, reassuring strength of a supporting beam directly beneath them. Eva flew across the roof like a cat.

They moved in tandem, as though tethered together by an invisible line. After reaching the end of the tiled roof, Eva vaulted up onto the neighboring building – a gymnast's leap of at least her own height. For one crazed, dissociated moment, Ivanov imagined her in another life, in another world, where Stalin and Beria were already dead, as they should have been, and cousin Carlo's little girl capered and played in the streets below. Perhaps she was a gymnast there, perhaps just a carefree child. But here, on the rooftops of Occupied Rome, she was a fugitive and his guide. She was almost certainly a killer as well, he reminded himself.

The special forces operative heaved himself up onto the next rooftop, taking considerably more care and time to execute the move than his diminutive pathfinder had. She was already running ahead of him.

This building was larger than the others and topped by a flat roof garden. Simple wooden furniture, trestle tables and benches were scattered about between huge pots containing herbs and simple vegetables like string beans and cucumbers. There was less of an imperative to track along in Eva's footsteps here, but he did so anyway. They moved quickly, covering the length of the building in half a minute.

He was wondering how they were going to cross the gap he could see looming ahead, when Eva accelerated toward it ... launching herself into the air like a triple jumper, or perhaps a parkour adept. She sailed across the void between the closely spaced apartment blocks, landing softly on the far side. Ivanov did not give himself a chance to hesitate or overthink the jump. His longer strides ate up the distance in a heart-beat. He shortened his last step by a few inches, flexed his knees and pistoned out into space. The gap was small, less than 4 feet across, but he felt his balls crawling up into his body as he sailed through clean air. Far below him, the hard, black cobblestones seemed to wait for him to miscalculate and fall.

He crunched down on the other side, rolling forward and coming up on the balls of his feet next to the little girl. She nodded as though he were a child who had passed a simple test.

They had landed on another flat roof, this one covered in washing lines from which sheets and blankets had been left to dry overnight. The bed clothes swayed in the soft breeze. Below, on the streets, the Red Army and NKVD paramilitary forces were kicking in doors, rousing the locals from their beds. A shot cracked out somewhere, followed by screams. First of terror, then of anger.

"Come Russian, we must move quickly."

Eva took off again, threading her way through the flapping laundry.

"Wait," said Ivanov. "Look ..."

He pointed to the south, where two gunships were hammering toward them. He could tell from their size and the deep percussive thrumming of the rotors that they were big monsters. Augmented-tech Mi-24s, at least one-and-a-half times the size of their uptime progenitors – partly because the Communists had not yet mastered post-industrial minimization, and partly because in Joseph Stalin's imagination, quantity had a quality all its own. These flying behemoths seemed to claw through the air, as though they might lose their grip on flight at any moment, so loaded down were they with armament and armor. As Eva turned to face the threat, crouching down, just like a cat on a ledge, columns of bright white light speared down from each of the choppers, searching and playing out over the city below with a strange, contrary beauty.

"They are heading right for us," said Eva. She did not panic, but he could hear the promise of it in her voice.

The gunships were reviled wherever they flew. As Ivanov and his new Roman guide watched, the nearer one opened up on some unknown target, pouring down a bright yellow ribbon of tracer fire; a neon stream of destruction fired into the heart of one of the oldest, most densely populated cities in Europe. Two seconds, the burst lasted, delivering 1000 rounds of alternating tracer, armor-piercing and high-explosive munitions. Smoke and flames rose from the impact point. The crash and rumble of collapsing masonry reached the two of them a second later.

Eva made as if to take off again and continue the headlong flight, as though they could simply outrun the airborne menace. Ivanov shot out one hand, grabbed the girl by the scruff of her neck and yanked her back – ripping a blanket from the nearest washing line and driving her down. The leading helicopter was closing on them fast. All four of its searchlights swept over the roofline of the church, three blocks away.

"Be still, be quiet," he commanded, on top of her now with the damp blanket covering them both. "And pray they do not have infrared sensors."

Of that at least he was reasonably sure. Had the gunships been fitted with FLIR or LLAMPS vision, the pilots would not have been using old-fashioned spot-lights. But you never knew. Perhaps they were just poorly trained.

The girl squirmed once underneath him, complaining that he was crushing her. But she lay silent and still as the miniguns roared and the cold white light crept along their rooftop.

Ivanov waited to die, hoping only that the shield of his body might afford Eva a false sense of security. Because in truth, if the gunners opened up on them, they would be shredded instantly.

He clutched the blanket tightly, grinding his teeth together, as the Mi-24 seemed to hover directly over-head. The downblast of the rotor wash tried to rip the cover away from them, and he could feel the little girl giving into her fears as violent tremors ran through her tiny frame. They endured a hell of sound and fury and supernova radiance ... and then it was gone. The flying beasts moved on and left them in darkness and relative quiet.

He waited a full minute before throwing back the blanket. His ears hummed and he blinked dust from his eyes, even though he had shut them tightly against the violent rotor wash and the glare of the searchlight.

"Come, Roman," he said gently to the girl. "We must hurry."

She stood up slowly and shakily. Ivanov watched on, impressed and somewhat saddened to see her cor-ral whatever fears had run wild, squeeze them all into a bitter little ball, and swallow it down.

"Yes," she agreed. "We must hurry."

She led off again and he followed her to the far corner of the building, where it all but kissed the corner of a neighboring apartment block. Eva stepped across the gap carefully, but her limbs were still shaking and she nearly lost her footing.

"Careful, little one," warned Ivanov, as he steadied her with a firm hand. "You are still in charge here. I need you to get us out of this."

The next building was possessed of a peaked roof, covered in terracotta tiles again, forcing him to attend to exactly where Eva was putting her feet. It was a difficult, anxious task, with the need to keep an eye out in case the helicopters swung back. For now, the Hinds seemed to be concentrating their search pattern around the part of the city where he had killed Borodin.

The Italian girl and her Russian charge ghosted across the roofline, crouched over, careful not to expose their silhouettes any more than was necessary. Ivanov could see a major gap coming up, and wondered whether he would be expected to make such a giant leap. But Eva pulled up before they reached the edge, turned to him and pointed to an old wooden ladder.

"Lay it across to the next building. It will reach."

It did, but the journey across was nerve-racking. The experience took him back to his earliest days of special forces training, when instructors had forced a young Pavel Ivanov and his fellow superheroes-in-waiting to perform any number of gravity-defying feats of life-threatening stupidity. He forced himself to forget the memories of one young friend who had fallen and snapped his spine like a twig. Best just to look ahead, keep the eyes level, breathe.

He stepped off the ladder just behind Eva, pulled it in toward them and lay it down carefully in the gutter. The building beneath them overlooked a small square, into which now drove an army truck and a BMP – an unwelcome sight that immediately had the rooftop pair crouch-scuffling around to the reverse slope. The helicopters were far enough off now that they could hear the crash of the truck's tailgate as a platoon of soldiers alighted, the crunch of their boots on the cobblestones, the shouts of officers and NCOs.

Eva and Ivanov stayed low and hidden on the lee side of the roofline, before dropping down onto a building next door, leaping across a small gap to the one beyond it, and repeating the trick with another ladder after that. Eventually the girl delivered them to a church overlooking a section of no-man's-land between the Allied and Soviet sectors. Work on the Roman Wall was incomplete here. A minefield and rows of razor wire still separated the different worlds, and here on the northern side of the divide, an armored personnel carrier idled away next to an incomplete guard tower. The soaring concrete battlements that bisected the ancient settlement elsewhere had not yet been raised here. Ivanov could see that the Communists had made inroads with earth-moving equipment, but they were still many months from completing one of the last links in the giant prison wall.

He leaned back against the steeply pitched roof of the old church, looking back to where they had come. Half of North Rome seemed to be blacked out. Fires burned here and there, and four gunships snarled and swooped and occasionally spat out long tongues of fire.

"I did all this?" Ivanov asked quietly.

A few steps ahead of him, Eva paused before edging her way around the belltower at the front of the church. "No, Russian, you did not do this," she replied. "Stalin did."

Having delivered her rebuke, she pushed on, leaving Ivanov to ponder where this girl had been and what she had done in her brief life to see so deeply into things. Eva Furedi – if that was her name – looked like she was only eleven or twelve years old, but it was possible, he supposed, that she'd had a few more years on the planet than that. She grew up in the postwar years, when food was scarce, even more so than now. Perhaps the urchin was a young woman. Or perhaps life in the slave city had simply squeezed all the youth from her at a very early age.

He carefully followed Eva around the tower installation, just as the troop carrier grunted and rumbled before suddenly lurching forward and driving off. He cursed softly and wondered aloud what was happening, and was surprised to be answered by a familiar voice.

"A pig can always be led to the smell of a tasty treat somewhere else."

Marius ... Ivanov cursed again, louder this time.

"Please, please," said the priest, from his comfortable repose, against the small twin to the tower around which the Russian had just edged. "The child does not need to hear such language."

Ivanov was about to point out that the child was one of the more ruthless females he had met since encountering the black widows of Chechnya, far off into the future. But he held his tongue. Eva was staring at

Marius with rapt attention. The Russian had seen that sort of devotion before. And it would've been oafish to speak ill of her. Ivanov owed her his life.

"So, where to now?" he asked instead.

"Into the light," said Marius, waving one hand toward the glitter and sparkle of Free Rome.

He reached down beside him and lifted up an old bolt-action rifle. Ivanov recognized the cumbersome attachment at the end of its muzzle: the priest intended to shoot a line over the Wall. Heavy black climber's rope ran down from the sabot into a small window of the belfry behind him.

Furedi braced himself and casually fired the weapon. Hundreds of meters of light, high-strength nylon twine snaked out across the gap between the divided city.

"It will take a moment for my brethren in the holy city to make fast the line." Even as he spoke, though, the rope went taut.

"The girl should go first," said Ivanov.

"The girl will stay here, Russian. With me. We have the Lord's work to do."

Ivanov started to protest, to insist that it would be too difficult and dangerous for her to remain undetected, with Skarov and Beria raking the city for any sign of him. He turned toward Eva to ask if she wanted to escape with him, but the girl was already gone. She had disappeared inside the belfry through another window.

"Bastards," Ivanov spat. "You would use a little girl—"

"Like you did?" Marius shot back, not unkindly. "You would not have escaped the city without her help, my friend. Without all of our help. Good men and women died for you today. They died for Rome and for their God, too, lest you feel you cannot bear the burden of their sacrifice alone. Eva Corleone has her part to play in God's design, as do we all. She will play her part here, with me. You have another path to walk."

The line was secure now. The priest tested it and nodded.

"But their lives were wasted," said Ivanov with real bitterness. "My mission was a failure."

Furedi shook his head and gestured for the Russian to come forward, as he slung a glider over the line.

"We have poked the bear today," said the priest. "Bled him well – a cut here, a cut there. Even the largest and most ferocious bear cannot sustain itself while it bleeds constantly. You did not achieve your goals perhaps. But we did well today, and those of us who died can go to our judgment knowing that we died well, for a good cause. For our city, and for God. Now go, Russian. Time is short."

Ivanov took a grip on the glider mechanism. He turned to speak to Marius one more time, but the priest gave him a push and out he sailed, away from the church tower and across the wasteland toward the free city.

13

South Rome (Allied sector)

While Plunkett guarded the entrance to the dining room, and Viv scouted the service lane behind Babington's as an escape route, Harry pushed Sobeskaia up against the wall again, next to a freezer unit. Kitchen staff gave them a wide berth. Harry was covered in blood, but then again the sight of blood was not unusual in a large commercial kitchen. The murderous look in his eyes was a little less commonplace, however.

"Comrade Sobeskaia," said Harry, as calmly as he could manage, "I am going to do my very best to get you out of here alive and in one piece, and back to the embassy with the nice Mr. Plunkett over there ..." He nodded to where the SIS agent had braced himself against the kitchen doors. "And Mr. Plunkett will then do his very best to make you disappear."

The short, rotund man, with a waxy sheen to his skin that seemed almost permanent, nodded gratefully. "Thank you, thank you," he began again.

Harry cut him off. "But first, just tell me: what the fuck is going on with the tungsten? It has to be something more than penetrator rounds or you wouldn't be here. You wouldn't be trying to get out and buy yourself a new life in the West."

Sobeskaia, who up until that point had looked merely terrified, now began to look both frightened and calculating.

"It is too much, too big," he replied. "I need debriefing in a safe place. I have much to tell."

Harry dug a thumb into the man's bicep to emphasize just who was controlling this negotiation.

"You won't get a chance to tell anybody anything until you get to a safe house, and I'm not taking you anywhere until I know whether it's worth it. Quite frankly, comrade, there's a very good chance I'm going to get my arse shot off tonight. It's a fine-looking arse, too. I spend a lot of time keeping it in trim and my girlfriend will be jolly fucking upset if some filthy Smedlov shoots a big bloody hole in it. So before we go anywhere, before you begin the first day of your new life as a pampered turncoat on some beach in bloody Australia, you're going to tell me everything you know. Just. In. Case."

The businessman grinned, or at least tried to. It was a weak, unconvincing effort. His eyes shifted left and right, and he jumped a little as the fire-exit door suddenly opened.

"Still looks clear out here, guv," reported St Clair.

"Thanks, Viv."

"Don't thank me, Your bloody Highness. Just make sure they pay my invoice promptly when I send it for this little bit of freelancing. Seven-day terms."

"Your check is in the mail."

Harry laid his gaze back on the quivering Sobeskaia, allowing the Russian to see the smile in his eyes die when he turned away from his old friend.

"Is complicated, and much difficulty," blurted Sobeskaia. "Much I do not know, much I have to tell. This is not place and, really, we must go now. I can tell all, later."

"Aggregate it for me, Comrade Huff Po."

Sobeskaia stared at him as if the prince had begun to speak a different language, which in a way he had. The argot of uptime. Harry found himself regressing to the future whenever he was stressed.

"What is the tungsten for?" Harry repeated. "What processes were you applying to it in your secret lair under the volcano or on the sea floor, or wherever the fuck it was you came from?"

He could hear renewed reports of discord and struggle over by the swinging doors to the dining area. He stole a quick glance over his shoulder and spied Plunkett fighting with an Asian-looking man who was about one-and-a-half times his size. The SIS agent was giving nothing away, though, matching his attacker blow for blow. The cocktail party beyond the doors seemed to have descended into chaos.

"Let's start with something you can answer, then," said Harry. "What the hell are you doing here? You were supposed to make contact with our people in North Rome, at your hotel. What happened with that?"

"I was betrayed. She was going to betray me, anyway," replied the Russian, looking genuinely bereft.

"This is your girlfriend, your mistress? The one who made contact with us initially?"

Sobeskaia nodded. "Anya. I loved her. We were going to escape together. But Beria got to her, turned her against me." His voice took on an unpleasant, wheedling edge. The fingernails-on-blackboard tone of a weak man whose failures were always someone else's fault.

"So you used her as a decoy. Sent her to a meeting you were supposed to make, and what, you scarpered off over here?"

"It was not like that," he protested. "She loved me, she did. But Beria forced her into betraying me. If I had gone with her to that meeting at the Grimaldi, I would have been captured, along with whoever you sent."

Ivanov, thought Harry. That would explain the fireworks on the dark side of the Wall. The one-time Spetznaz officer had either walked into a trap, or seen it and sprung it early. Harry shook his head. There were days when operating downtime was not just frustrating, but life-threatening. Little or no satellite cover, scant overwatch, if any at all, and the most primitive of extraction procedures. A gun, some directions, and a pat on the back for good luck.

"What were you going to tell our man?" Harry asked. "We had the tungsten shavings already. You must have had more to say. And you're not leaving until I get it, now."

Plunkett appeared at his elbow, bruised and bleeding from a cut to his scalp, his shirt and jacket torn. But he was upright and moving. The man he had been fighting was not. Harry took a quick sight picture of the chaos and madness now spreading into the kitchen. Plunkett's NKVD opponent was lying on the tiles, his head neatly split by a meat cleaver.

"Things have gone a bit wobbly, I'm afraid," he said. "Best we get a move on."

"St Clair is keeping an eye on the service lane," said Harry. "It's clear for now. We can get out through there if you can organize some cover for us. It looked like there was half a regiment of Beria's finest loitering around out the front. Be sure to have some of your lads covering the rear as well. Or they will very soon."

"As I said before, I'll see what I can do," replied Plunkett with forced patience, before absenting himself again.

"You heard the man, Sobeskaia. We'll see what we can do – and we'll do what we can. But not until I know it's worth it. Or that *you* are worth it. What is Beria doing with all the tungsten? If it's being run through the Functional Projects Bureau, it won't be something simple like armor-piercing rounds."

The defector seemed to weigh up his options and find them wanting. He took a deep breath, which came out in a loose ragged rush.

"It is big," he said. "Everything is so big with this. The production schedules, they are not possible for us. But Beria, he will not listen. Three of my best foremen have gone to the gulag now because they have failed to deliver on schedule."

Harry resisted the urge to cock an eyebrow at that. Sobeskaia almost certainly selected the names of those foremen, to avoid a spell at the gulag himself. Cheap shitty toasters and blame-shifting were the two areas where Soviet production methods led the world.

"Keep talking," he said, as St Clair stuck his head back in the kitchen.

"Got some movement out here, governor."

"You going to be all right, Viv?"

The commando-turned-businessman smiled and extracted a Metalstorm P50 personal weapon from the voluminous interior of his dinner jacket.

"Wish I'd thought of that," said Harry.

The P50 was an uptime model composed of exotic composites and ceramics. Only a few dozen of them came through the Transition, as best he knew. St Clair had almost certainly stolen his. It would not have registered on the primitive metal detectors employed by embassy security to pick up junk like Makarov pistols.

"Carry on then," said Harry, shifting his attention back to Sobeskaia. "You were telling me about the production schedules. What else is so big about this project?"

"Big in all ways. These things they want – tungsten rods – they are huge, like telephone pole. But the machining is precise. Tolerances too great for my equipment and workers. I do not choose my workers, you understand. They are sent to me, many of them."

"Oh, I understand the concept of slave factories, Mr. Sobeskaia, don't worry about that. Just tell me about the rods." A queasy tension had taken a grip on Harry's stomach, though. It grew worse as the *boyar* spoke.

"I do not know what for Beria needs these giant rods," he said. "I am only part of the production process. At Prozpekt Elektric, we provide machined rods to specification, or else. It is bad enough when I have to provide hundreds. But now they want thousands – *tens of thousands*."

Harry's balls tried to crawl up inside his body and his stomach did a slow flip forward. "The machining of the tungsten rods, what did that involve?" he asked. "What did you have to do to them?"

Sobeskaia tried to wave him away. "It is a complicated thing."

"Pretend I am a simple man. One who could do you a great deal of harm. Like Stalin, for instance. Pretend you are explaining to Comrade Stalin what you have to do in his very special, secret factory. Explain to the maximum psychopath why you, Comrade Sobeskaia, need more of his money and his slaves to give him what he wants."

The defector appeared to be more than a little perturbed by the idea of having to explain himself to Joseph Stalin. He looked as though even imagining the encounter could be fatal.

"The rods," he started to explain, slowly and carefully, "are 6.1 meters long, 30 centimeters in diameter, and solid except for a pair of centimeter-wide shafts running from base of the rod to small chamber 1 meter from nose cone."

"Nose cone?" Harry said, growing ever more alarmed.

"Of a sort. It is really more of the tapering effect. But this is not all. I am also to place four channels at the base of the model. Each one to be at a point same distance from each other ..." He seemed to struggle for words now.

"Equidistant," prompted Harry. "Equidistant from each other. Like the stabilizing fins on a missile."

"Yes," said Sobeskaia, staring at him and nodding slowly. "Just like a missile."

"Okay, I think I've heard enough. You've earned your get-out-of-jail-free card."

He reached up to his ear, unconsciously looking for a press-to-talk headset. *Damn it ...*

He was not plugged into the matrix here. He could not call down air support, or extraction, or back-up. Not without physically searching out the people he needed to talk to. He thought he had got over that habit after so many years in the past. Apparently not.

"Wait here. No. Come with me."

He took Sobeskaia by the arm and gave him a push, a little more gently this time, toward Plunkett, who was talking into an old-fashioned phone attached to the wall on the far side of the kitchen. Restaurant staff were still running about, jabbering at each other, all panicking at the mess in the dining room. Plunkett saw him coming and hung up.

"We'll have a car here in four minutes," he promised. "I can take care of our guest after that, if you wish. Or would you like to ride along?"

A wave of exhaustion rolled over Harry. "What I would like to do is track down my girlfriend, who is fast losing patience with me, have myself a hot bath and a cold drink, and fall into bed with her."

Sobeskaia looked alarmed at the thought.

"But I can see our new best friend here won't be having that," Harry continued, "so I guess we'll just crack on, shall we?"

"Yes, let's," said Plunkett.

Three of his people pushed through the swing doors, as if summoned at that moment. Two men, one woman, all looking severely disheveled. They took up station around Sobeskaia, unshipped their weapons – no inconvenient restrictions for them, Harry noted – and at a gesture from Plunkett, they all moved toward the exit.

"How did the party go out there?" said Harry. "I'm afraid I had to leave early."

"Oh, too bad," replied Plunkett. "You probably didn't miss much, though. We had the most awful gatecrashers."

Stalin's Hammer: Rome is over

Prince Harry will return in *Stalin's Hammer: Cairo.*

Lightning Source UK Ltd.
Milton Keynes UK
UKOW02f0756070315

247455UK00001B/8/P